Finding the Right Girl

A Nice *GUY* to Love Spin-Off Novel

❧

VIOLET DUKE

❧

Copyright © 2013 Violet Duke

All rights reserved. Except as permitted under the U.S. Copyright Act of 1976, this book and any portion thereof may not be reproduced, scanned, transferred, or distributed in any print or electronic form without the express written permission of the author. Participation in any aspect of piracy of copyrighted materials, inclusive of the obtainment of this book through non-retail or other unauthorized means, is in actionable violation of the author's rights.

This is a work of fiction. Names, characters, businesses, media, brands, places, and incidents are either the products of the author's imagination or used fictitiously. The author acknowledges the trademarked status and registered trademark owners of all branded names referenced without TM, SM, or (R) symbols due to formatting constraints, and is not claiming ownership of or collaboration with said trademark brands. Any resemblance to actual persons, living or dead, or events is purely coincidental.

Copyedits by Mickey Reed Editing and C&C Editing Services
Cover design by Violet Duke
Excerpt from *Rebel* © 2014 Skye Jordan
Excerpt from *A Maine Christmas...or Two* © 2013 J.S. Scott

ISBN: 0989163393
ISBN-13: 978-0-9891633-9-2

Printed in the United States of America

10 9 8 7 6 5 4 3 2 1

DEDICATION

To my parents, my in-laws, and of course
my MVD (Mr. Violet Duke).

Without each of you, I'd just be a crazy person with a whole lot of stories in her head…and complete chaos in her life. You all make it possible for me to be an author.

.

Book Description

Brian Sullivan has been in love twice in his lifetime. He lost his first love to early-onset Huntington's, and he lost the other more recently...to his brother. And somehow, his heart has managed to heal itself after both. Amazingly, without therapy. That doesn't mean he hasn't gotten more wary along the way, however. In fact, he's been thinking lately that maybe his brother's now retired nothing-but-flings rule isn't such a bad idea. Unfortunately, being the nice guy poster boy and all, Brian isn't exactly versed in the fine art of flings. So he looks to the outrageously 'unique,' provokingly *button-pushing* Tessa Daniels for a crash course.

There's absolutely no way he's falling in love with this one...right?

Tessa has no idea what she was thinking telling Brian that she was some sort of fling expert. She's never been flung before and she sure as heck doesn't know where or how to begin flinging a guy like Brian. It was a temporary lapse in sanity, really—no doubt because of the can't-help-but-fall-for-him brain fuzz that hits her whenever he's around. Not only does the man have her being more herself than she's ever been in her life, but he's the only person she knows who seems to have as many demons and skeletons in the closet as she does. What's more, he's got her thinking of the one thing she stopped letting herself even hope for years ago.

A happily ever after.

CHAPTER ONE

"Purple *again*? Why don't you ever put *green* in your hair, Tessa? Green's my favorite."

As always, Tessa Daniels felt her heart tug at the slight w-lisp she could hear curled into Jilly's use of the word 'green.' Because adorable as it was, Tessa had no doubt that lisp would've been gone by now had the sweet young girl sitting across from her not spent the last few years missing long stretches of school days from all her complications with Juvenile Huntington's Disease.

She was only six-years old.

Sweeping her purple-tipped hair up into a ponytail, Tessa went over to sit on the edge of Jilly's newly installed hospital bed. It was one of the three dozen new top-of-the-line beds now housed here, thanks to the grant money she and her friend Connor had managed to secure for the care home his sister-in-law had lived out her Huntington's end-stage in.

"Green? I thought your favorite color was rainbow, Jilly-bean."

"You made a rhyme!" giggled Jilly, trying and valiantly succeeding in softly clapping together her two little hands, despite the near-frozen curved angle of her fingers preventing her palms from making solid contact with one another.

Seeing the rigidity of Jilly's limbs and fingers—the worst case Tessa had ever seen in all her years of volunteer work with those plagued with the juvenile and adult forms of HD—tore another jagged shard out of Tessa's heart.

Damn this disease.

"I've never been able to find a green hair dye that'll show on my dark hair," answered Tessa belatedly. "But now I'll be sure to look even harder." She grabbed the small tub of crayons and poured it out on the activity tray that hooked onto the side of Jilly's bed. "Which color green do you like better, the darker ones or the lighter ones?"

Jilly took a long, serious look at the crayons, sifting through them with her splayed fingers, poking at and then dismissing various colors of green with her pinky.

Tessa couldn't help but smile a proud, albeit sad smile when Jilly used her thumb to expertly flip one of the crayons up by its sharpened tip and catch it between two of her fingers. Every day in all these little ways, Jilly was showing herself to be so incredibly adaptive to the increasing stiffness in her extremities due to her JHD.

"Slick move there. Did your physical therapist show you that one?"

"Nope, I learned it all by myself," beamed Jilly as she held up the chosen crayon, wedged between her index and middle finger as one would hold a cigarette. "I like *this* one the best."

"Oh man!" Tessa feigned horror and put the bright green crayon up to her hair. "Neon green? I'll look like a glowing alien with neon green stripes in my hair."

"You'll look like a mermaid princess!" squealed Jilly, bopping happily in her bed. "I can't wait to see it!"

That was yet another thing Tessa admired about Jilly.

The happy little girl simply did not live her life in maybes; she believed in things with her whole heart, and looked forward to that assured reality with all the confidence in the world.

"Okay, neon green it is," promised Tessa, angling the tub off the edge of the tray so Jilly could slide the crayons back into it. It would have taken a fifth of the time to just scoop up the crayons herself, but Tessa had learned long ago not to rob anyone with JHD of any task they could accomplish on their own. "So what do you want to do first today? Do you want to take a cruise around the courtyard and hang out in the garden or play a round of video games?"

"Video games!"

Of course.

Smiling, Tessa pulled a little video game cartridge out of her pocket and let Jilly screech excitedly over the new game while she set the TV and modified controllers up for them to play head-to-head.

"This is the exact game I wanted! How did you know?" Unable to sit still, Jilly was practically bouncing off the walls as Tessa clicked in the new cartridge.

"You remember my friend Connor? His niece Skylar recommended it. Her best friend's little brother is your age and he said this game is the talk of the playground." Tessa slid the comfier of the two chairs in the room over and settled in next to Jilly—this was no doubt going to go on for a while. "And unfortunately for you, missy, Skylar gave me a few pointers on how to totally own you at this game."

A fierce little glint lit up Jilly's eyes. "If I win, I get to pick the movie we watch today."

"Whoa, we're playing high-stakes, are we?" Tessa made a show of eyeing her pint-sized opponent up and down. "Okay, Jilly-bean, you've got yourself a deal."

As they shook hands, Tessa had a quick flashback to a similar handshake agreement they'd had months ago, when a very mulish Jilly had demanded that Tessa stop letting her win at everything. Or else.

Lordy, she loved this tiny little miracle to pieces.

They quickly got down to business and not even two minutes into the game, Tessa already knew that it was going to be a princess movie kind of afternoon.

◈

BRIAN SULLIVAN STOPPED and stared at the photo of his wife up on the memory wall of the care home in Cactus Creek where she'd spent the last few years of her life. It was a photo from when she'd first been admitted, a far cry from the pictures of her that were forever burned into his memories—candid snapshots his mind held on to from the first day he'd laid eyes on her back in high school, and the even more different memories of the final, of many, times he'd been forced to say goodbye to her. Beth had only been twenty-eight when she died, but her decade-long battle with JHD had aged her far more than was fair in pain and suffering. Ditto on its effect on him and his daughter as well.

Damn that disease.

He hadn't been back to the care home for over three years—not since Beth's funeral. But he'd made a point to come in today to drop off a gift for one of Beth's favorite nurses on her last day before she retired. The amazing woman had saved Beth's life on at least a dozen occasions during her time there.

After one last look, he turned and left the patient wing. But instead of heading back to his car, he found himself walking through the courtyard over to the back garden area. His wife used to love sitting out there and feeling the sun on her skin. Even after she'd stopped remembering his name and then eventually stopped recognizing him altogether, there were times when he'd come by to visit her and she'd immediately point at her wheelchair and smile. He had doggedly clung to the hope that some part of her brain seemed to remember that he would take her out back and sit with her.

At least that's what he used to tell himself on the really bad days when she'd look at him not just in confusion, but in fear. When he'd hear her gurgle out a panicked stranger-danger cry, which would break his heart every single time.

He sat and replayed the memories as he gazed out at the craggy mountainous landscape just beyond the fenced garden of the care facility. Random giant cactuses standing head and shoulders above trees that looked deceptively like tall, unkempt grass from afar, dried in every shade of green under the sun. His eyes wandered aimlessly, restlessly over it all—until a splash of electric color in stunning contrast to the rugged, red dirt backdrop drew his focus like a magnet and had him doing a jarring double-take.

Squinting, he eyed the t-shirt and shorts-clad figure venturing into the deep pockets of the mountainside, dips and hollows that carved out valleys most folks would never know existed under the camouflage of the arid overgrowth all around.

Had to be that his mind was playing tricks on him. A dainty little pixie with peekaboo strips of neon-bright rocker hair out in that terrain?

Couldn't be.

But it was. That was definitely another flash of sexy hot

purple he just saw.

And for some reason, the streaks of color in the long ponytail of ink-black hair disappearing farther into the desert brush immediately had him thinking of the woman who'd been making random cameos in his thoughts for months now, since the day of his brother Connor's wedding.

Shockingly pink highlights, a fallen angel smile, and a laugh he'd been unable to forget.

He shook his head—partly to try and dislodge the image of her out of his mind—and studied the hiker intently when she happened to turn in his direction for a brief second. Just long enough for him to see her face fully.

Huh, what were the odds? Same woman.

Now what the hell was she doing hiking out there in a pair of backless sneakers and an utterly useless-in-the-mountains slouched, boho-gypsy looking bag, similar to the one his daughter had asked him for this past Christmas?

He rolled his eyes. The woman took offbeat to a whole new level.

Before he could even decide whether or not to follow her so he could tell her as much, however, she dropped out of sight.

Literally. Dropped.

With an explosive curse, he went tearing across the lawn, hopping over the fence to make his way up the mountain to find the hidden ravine she must have fallen down into.

∞§∞

UN-FREAKIN-BELIEVABLE!

Tessa unstrangled herself from the noose her bag strap was making around her neck and untangled her now-ripped clothing from the thicket of mesquite and ironwood trees she'd crashed through on her plummet down. The small gulch had appeared out of nowhere. One minute there'd been ground under her feet and the next she was falling like a coin down a slot.

When the rustling ruckus of her fall eventually dissipated, blanketing her in the quiet of the surprisingly lush desert forest once again, that's when she finally heard it.

The garbled grunts and snorts of a creature not twenty feet away from her.

Scrabbling quietly to a steadier perch on the tree that had broken her final descent, she took a good look down. All but camouflaged in the shadows below was an animal she'd never seen before that looked like a cross between a boar and a huge possum. If not for the viciously long tusks, the creature could've even looked cute. Cuddly.

She quickly retracted that assessment when the hair on the animal's body shot up like spikes and a hot, angry snarl hissed out of him.

Javelina. Almost twenty-eight years in Arizona now and not once had she ever seen a Javelina in person.

Who said there was no such thing as small miracles?

Tessa stopped moving altogether and quickly took inventory of her surroundings and situation. She was in a tree and injured...check. More checks sounded in her head as she raced through her options and limitations. She'd almost landed on her plan for escape when she heard a muffled voice shout out from above, "*Tessa!* Are you okay?"

That voice. She knew that voice. It was a voice her subconscious seemed particularly fond of—if her insanely overheated dreams over the past few months were any indication.

Brian Sullivan. Brian Sullivan was here and calling out her name in that wickedly deep alpha male voice of his.

Hot damn, her subconscious was definitely recording that one to put on instant replay later.

Much later.

When she wasn't one big walking bruise with a giant thorny branch crammed against her butt cheeks and a vicious, growling animal not far away.

A snap of dry twigs alerted her attention back down the ravine.

Crap. Okay, make that *two* vicious, growling animals.

She added a perfectly reasonable freak-out over the situation as another thing she'd put on hold until later. Ignoring the twenty different kinds of pain attacking her brain from all her injuries, she scanned the gulch wall she'd tumbled down and spidey-sprang to the surface with the least amount of cacti and succulents, tucking and rolling when her ninja skills proved to be seriously lacking.

Brian grabbed her by the shirt to keep her from sliding back down the gulch at the very last second. Then he growled in her ear, "*Climb!*"

◈

OPTING FOR THE ROUTE that'd get them a safe distance away from the javelina the fastest, Brian forcibly shoved Tessa up the ravine wall with the steepest angle. Scrappy little thing. She was surprisingly quick in her ascent up the rocky terrain, considering how bad of a tumble she'd just taken.

Keeping his ears open for the sound of the javelina charging after them, Brian didn't let up for a moment until he had the top ridge of the gulch in his sights.

What had his blood pressure shooting back through the roof again, however, was seeing the dainty little hand covered in dirt and blood reaching out to him from above.

Grabbing hold of a thick tree root jutting out of the mountain instead, he hoisted himself up and over the edge.

He paused to catch his breath, allowing the adrenaline to drain out of his system as he watched her smile at him in relief and scoot her way back from the edge of the cliff.

She'd had her legs wrapped around a tree to brace herself.

So she *wasn't* completely insane.

That meant the jury was only out on him now.

Here they were, just having scrambled their way up a steep ravine to avoid a pair of rabid javelina and his brain was thinking about how it would feel to have those sexy legs of hers wrapped around him instead.

He was definitely the one losing his mind.

It took a few silent minutes of their walking from the trails back to the care facility lawn for him to finally notice all the deep, gouging scrapes and gashes slashed across her calves and thighs. "*Shit*, you're bleeding. Come here, let me—"

She jumped back and gave him a look. Not a wary one but one that looked…confused. Out of sorts.

Maybe she'd hit her head when she fell.

"I'm fine." She backed up again when he took another step forward.

There was that look again. Like she was expecting him to suddenly sprout a second or third head.

"Thanks for coming to my rescue back there, Brian. I really appreciate it. But really, you don't have to do this 'knight in shining armor' thing. I'm good."

He could see that. There wasn't a single thing about her

that cried out 'damsel in distress,' even given what could've happened to her back there. She wasn't a leaf shaking in the wind over it, and it wasn't because she was just made of tougher stuff either; he could see the weary, still-simmering terror in her eyes. She wasn't over the situation by a longshot—she just appeared...acceptant of it. Simple as that.

And that intrigued him as much as it rankled. He remembered how devastated she'd looked at the wedding when she'd told him how she lost her sister to Huntington's. He knew that devastation, knew exactly what that kind of loss did to a person. Simple acceptance was the last thing he'd expect from her.

The one thing he'd yet to be able to achieve himself.

"Why didn't you scream?"

"What?" She looked up in surprise.

"When you fell, and when you saw the javelina—you didn't scream. Not even a little. Why not?" He had to know.

She blinked as if the question, and the reason, had never occurred to her. Her shoulder lifted and fell in a no-nonsense shrug as she said simply, "I didn't think anyone would come."

When she smothered a pained wince as she bent down to get her keys from her now tattered bag on the ground, he reached for her again, not wanting her to go with an intensity that stunned him.

"Turn around." He tried gentling his voice. "Let me check out your legs."

Smooth, Sullivan. Real smooth.

At least that made her stop backing away from him though. Of course now she was just staring at him like he was nuts. "Let me check out your *injuries*," he amended. "I have a first-aid kit in my car."

"Oh. That's okay, so do I." She was back to cutting

quickly across the lawn. Three more stealthy steps back. "I have a whole survival kit in there, in fact," she continued on a cute ramble, "complete with food for a week, extra changes of clothes, and a small generator. I even have a SAM splint and one of those foldable pocket walking canes in case I break a leg or something."

Well that was…unexpected. Brian wasn't quite sure how to respond to that. "Are you some sort of apocalypse radical or just on the lam from the authorities?"

Yeah…he should've just kept his mouth shut. The woman rattled him, infected him with that talking-out-of-his-ass virus he hadn't had since he was a teen.

For some reason, however, that especially asinine comment succeeded in making her stop retreating. And laugh.

That laugh.

It was like hearing a Christmas carol on the hottest day of summer.

"I almost forgot how much I like you, Brian."

Likewise.

"Listen, thanks again for saving me, but I really do have to run. I'll ask Connor for your number and take you out for coffee sometime. Or pie!" She grinned. "Pie is better as a thank-you."

Then she turned and ran off to the parking lot, leaving Brian to stand there and simply stare at her long ponytail windmilling around with every buoyant step she took.

The fact that she stopped suddenly and spun around at the edge of the lot to give him a final smiling wave had him completely off-kilter. She was freakin' adorable as hell.

And absolutely, positively the last woman on earth he pictured himself being *this* drawn in by.

CHAPTER TWO

BRIAN GRABBED a bag of tortilla chips from the pantry and checked Connor's fridge for some fresh guacamole. He knew Abby had a big presentation this past week with the intertribal education board members on her most recent research recommendations so he knew she had to have made a vat of guac to munch on while she'd prepared.

Jackpot. He swiped the familiar glass tupperware off the top shelf and dug in.

"Don't you have food at your own house?" complained Connor as he entered the kitchen.

"Not since you went and married my best friend," complained Brian right back. He sighed in mock melancholy. "Abby's guac used to be in *my* fridge every week. Not to mention the homemade cookies and all these great sandwiches she'd make for me to take for lunch." At the fond reminders, his next sigh was less feigned. And utterly silent.

While he was definitely thrilled to have Abby as a sister-in-law now, he missed how close they used to be. Not that he ever mentioned that fact to Connor or Abby. Even though he really was truly over his non-platonic feelings for her, any and all conversations on the topic generally ended up being pretty awkward for all involved, so he avoided it altogether.

"Nice of you to say hi before you raided my kitchen by the way." Connor checked the time. "Tell me you haven't been here since school let out."

Brian saluted him with a loaded chip as a non-apologetic hello. "I just got here. Today's faculty meeting was short. And since it's my turn to take Skylar and Becky out for Friday night dinner, I'm just killing time until they're done with musical theatre club rehearsals." He looked around for the remote. Connor had a way better satellite sports channel package than he did. "I didn't even know you were home. Where's your car?"

"Abby took the Lexus to work since her car is in the shop again. I came home to get my tux and Abby's dress for tonight. We've got another fundraising benefit to go to."

"And you're not concocting some excuse to get out of it?" Weird. Connor usually hated going to those functions.

"This isn't for work. It's for one of the charities Tessa and I have been helping out."

At the mere mention of Tessa's name, Brian's hunt for the remote was instantly forgotten. Carefully keeping his voice neutral, he launched a very *casual* interrogation. "Tessa...that's your caterer friend right? The one with the pink-striped hair? What's the deal with her? Why'd you end up picking a cook to help you with all your pro bono grant write-ups?"

"Because she's damn good at it. Besides, the catering thing is just a part-time gig for Tessa and Lana. Lana started the catering company and asked Tessa to partner in because of all her dessert-making experience. Once upon a time, Tessa worked at a bakery for maybe five years, I think. But just like Lana, Tessa also has a day job. She's the chief editor of the two sister magazines, *AZ Hotspots* and *AZ Potluck*."

Brian was impressed. He knew of both those local magazines; the seasonal travel magazine was his standard reading material of choice in every doctor's waiting room he's sat in for the past few years, and he knew for a fact that the online cooking magazine was a huge hit with his colleagues at school. This Tessa was just full of surprises.

Feeling Connor quietly studying him, Brian looked up. "What?"

"You're into her, aren't you?"

"Who? The odd, opinionated woman who thought it was a good idea to have my daughter hack away at some fruits with a gigantic cooking knife at your wedding reception as a means to get her over her fear of knives? Fully aware that I'd bust a nut if I found out about it?"

Connor arched a knowing eyebrow.

Brian grunted and turned to grab a soda from the fridge. "Yeah. A little bit."

༄

HE WAS STILL THINKING about that 'little bit' the next day on his Saturday morning run. With Beth having been his high school sweetheart, and Abby being the only other woman he'd ever had any feelings for, Brian had a sorely limited dating experience database to draw on to analyze the matter.

"Maybe Connor had the right idea all along," he muttered to himself as he hit the two mile mark and turned around to head back. He'd dogged Connor constantly about being a man whore with his one-month fling rule, but look how it ended up. He got the girl, and he'd never lacked for female company all the way up until then.

Visions of Tessa began swimming around in his head then—images of that stubborn frown of hers that seemed to come as a combo pack with her dancing, dark-as-night eyes. It went hand in hand with the inexplicably cute way she seemed to just say exactly what she was thinking.

And that killer smile...

No.

A girl like that wouldn't be into casual flings. For all he knew, she already had someone she went home to every night.

Hitting the last mile mark, he pounded down harder on the pavement at a near sprint back to his house. Mostly to stamp out the feelings of jealousy crawling up his spine.

He had to stop thinking about the woman.

Yanking the iPod velcro strap off his bicep as he toed his sneakers off, he called out to see if Skylar was awake yet.

Silence.

Not surprising. The kid had spent most of the night on the phone with her BFF-since-daycare. And this was *after* he'd taken the girls out for pizza and ice cream. Seriously, the two were inseparable all week in school as well as every weekend at each other's homes on alternating sleepovers—how on earth they still had things left to talk about on the phone was beyond him.

He grabbed a quick shower and set out with grand plans for cooking up a big breakfast instead of his usual cereal and sliced fruit specialty. He rocked that culinary masterpiece something fierce. Lately, however, Skylar seemed to be getting a little fancy in her taste palate. Probably from watching all those cooking shows she seemed to be into now.

As he passed Skylar's still-closed door, he heard her talking quietly on the other side.

Geez, how much could two thirteen-year-olds possibly

have to discuss?

But then he heard something that made him stop in his tracks.

That laugh.

Every single time he heard it, he was reminded of how long it'd been since he'd laughed like that. As if the universe wasn't at times cruel and unyielding. As if the heart didn't have limits to how much pain and disappointment it could take.

Then the next words he heard had him flipping his lid and grabbing for her door knob.

"Have you checked out those websites I told you about for the HD gene testing—"

"Skylar," he thundered, using his break-only-in-case-of-emergency voice to breach her privacy without knocking first. "What's going on in here?" His gaze sliced over to Skylar's computer and the woman staring at him from the Skype screen. *Tessa.* When her face lit up just the tiniest bit for a split-second before quickly shifting to a calm, diplomatic smile—as if she hadn't just been advising his daughter on a life-changing gene test, while looking as distractingly soft and sweet as ever—he felt his blood pressure shoot through the roof in two different directions.

"Hi dad," hazarded Skylar carefully. "You remember Tessa, right? Uncle Connor's friend from the wedding?"

Jaw locked, he merely nodded, keeping his eyes trained on Tessa.

Who took that moment to wave at him.

Good lord, the woman knew how to push his buttons without even trying. "Skylar, since when do you skype your uncle's friends about your private health matters?"

...Matters that they'd already decided *against*.

"Dad, she knows so much about this gene testing stuff. I was just asking her some questions."

"Questions that should come straight to me or your doctor, or even your therapist." He shot a pointed look at the screen. "Not to random adults you met once a few months ago."

"Actually, we've talked a bunch of times since then over at Uncle Connor's house—"

"Skylar," Tessa broke in, "I think it might be a good idea for me to log off now because frankly, I'm a little worried my staying online is going to give your dad an ulcer." She turned back to stare him straight in the eye then, locking horns with him as she added, "But feel free to skype me again anytime. You can ask me anything you want about the HD testing."

Brian bristled. Clearly, the woman wasn't *that* concerned about his stomach lining.

The screen blipped out to black and he swung his gaze back over to his daughter.

He didn't even know where to begin.

Thankfully, the faint chirping of Skylar's cell phone gave him a brief moment to put a lid on his temper and gather his thoughts. After all, it wasn't Skylar he was pissed at.

"It's Tessa."

Exactly.

No wait, what? He looked up and saw Skylar waving her phone at him. "It's a text from Tessa. She wrote, '*TELL YOUR DAD I'D LIKE HIM TO MEET ME FOR LUNCH OR DINNER ONE OF THESE DAYS SO WE CAN DISCUSS THIS. ANYWHERE HE WANTS, ANYTIME. HIS CHOICE.*'" Skylar shrugged and gave him a wide take-it-up-with-management smile.

Another chirp.

"Um…"

"What does it say?" he barked.

"She texted, and I'm totally quoting her here, '*FIGURED THIS WAY HE CAN'T SAY NO.*' End quote." Her teeth flashed again as she gave him an innocent look. "That text was probably just for me."

Great. Now Skylar was looking thoroughly entertained by the situation.

Another innocuous double blink. "Why don't you meet Tessa tonight? I'll be leaving for Becky's right after lunch and won't be back until late tomorrow."

He knew she offered the oh-so-helpful comment just to keep him from being a hermit all weekend, but his now unruly imagination was having a field day with the suggestion.

"Fine," he ground out. "She and I may as well hash this out as soon as possible." *Uh-huh, whatever you need to tell yourself, buddy.* "Tell her dinner, 6:30 at the Italian restaurant the block over from her street."

With a slow smile, Skylar tilted her head over to a do-tell angle. "How do you know what street Tessa lives on?"

Dammit. Busted. "Your uncle mentioned it. Just text her back, will you?"

She bit her lip to hide her grin when the chirping reply came back moments later.

He waited, not at all patiently.

"Errr..." Her voice was now brimming with humor. "Tessa wrote back, '*I PROBABLY WON'T BE HUNGRY THAT EARLY BUT THEY HAVE A GREAT HAPPY HOUR SO TELL HIM TO GO FOR IT. I'LL BE THERE AT SEVEN. BYE!*' Then a smiley face."

Of all the aggravating... "Why'd she even ask me to pick a time then? And does she honestly expect me to get there a half hour before she does?"

Actually...he wouldn't put it past her.

So. Unbelievably. Weird.

He didn't want to even think about what his reluctantly growing fascination over her little quirks said about *him*.

"Wow, she really gets your fish frying, doesn't she?" remarked Skylar, using one of Abby's trademark sayings with a touch of awe.

A harmless observation with a little too much female insight for his comfort level.

"Cereal and fruits in five minutes," he muttered and stalked out of her room.

When he heard another chirp followed by a smothered giggle, he just kept right on walking.

It was undoubtedly safer that way.

❦

TESSA PACED around her living room as the ticking clock on her wall got closer and closer to her scheduled "discussion dinner" with Brian. She wasn't calling it a date; her nerves would never survive the night if she did.

She hadn't been able to stop replaying the way he'd called out her name down in the ravine. The man was just so distractingly brawny. Bearlike. But gentle. And caring. She'd counted three instances when his protective instincts had overruled all else that day, and his voice had dropped down to this rough, untamed rasp that had her wanting to jump on him and bury her face against his throat so she could drink in all that ruggedness.

A dizzying wave of heat washed over her at the memory.

Geez, she needed to get a grip.

Finally, she couldn't take it anymore. When her clock hit

5:30, she grabbed her car keys and headed out the door.

She pulled into the lumber yard a short while later, just as the sales office was closing.

"Hey, Frank!" she called out, waving her goodbyes to the workers who were calling it a day.

Frank's bushy white eyebrows hopped up with delight. "Hey dollface, what's shakin'?"

"Nothing much. Just thought I'd stop by and drop off your favorite."

"Hot damn, I was hoping you'd come visit this week. Jackie's been on a steamed fish kick for days." He rolled his eyes. "Lucky thing she adores you because these hotdog runs are the only times she lets me cheat."

Tessa covered up her grin. If only he knew that the 'hotdog' he loved so much was really a specialty dog from her favorite hotdog joint, made with extra-lean ground meat, fennel, and a mix of ground eggplant and mushrooms. The only other one in on the secret was Frank's wife, who purposely never let him go to the hotdog restaurant in question so he'd never know that his one indulgence was actually not all that bad for him.

Frank quickly unwrapped the hotdog, loaded with all the fixings, and took a huge bite.

"Lord, that's good."

Smiling, she took her matching order and headed out to the back door.

"Sweets, be sure to keep to the cedar stacks. Hank stacked those. We had the new kid working the forklift today." He shook his head tiredly. "Lord have mercy. Boy was as cockeyed as they come. Took him all day and the wood still wasn't lined up straight. Wouldn't trust any of those stacks to climb on."

"Got it. Thanks, Frank!" The cedar planks were her favorites anyway, which she suspected was why he always had Hank stack those. "I'll be down before you leave."

While cutting across the gigantic lumber yard to the tallest cedar stack, Tessa stuffed the hotdog bag into her new slouch bag—the old one was still in the accessory ICU after her fall the other day—so she'd have her hands free to climb. Though she was still a little achy from her bumps and bruises, the climb was quick-going. And once up on top, she turned in a slow three-sixty to gaze at the landscape all around before settling down in the middle, facing west, to watch the sun start to set.

While most folks she knew loved their tropical paradises or snowy retreats, Tessa had always thought the rough beauty of Arizona at sunset trumped them all. The entire desert canvas painted with the rich, earthy colors that never failed to ground her, and clear skies blasted with vibrant colors spinning the entire color wheel. It was a feast for her eyes to see everything around her become so primitively alive, before drifting off to sleep for the night. The desert just had a rough sort of beauty that had always spoken to her, healed her just as it rejuvenated her in even her toughest times.

And sometimes, when she looked over to her right and the sunlight was hitting just so, she could still see her father and sister sitting right there with her.

God, she missed them.

CHAPTER THREE

AT 7 PM ON THE DOT, Tessa walked into the small Italian eatery and found Brian leaning against the wall near the entrance, looking like Johnny Lumberjack with his sexy, golden brown hair and scruffy five o'clock shadow. When he spotted her, he smiled—the first smile he'd ever directed her way, she realized...and she nearly swallowed her tongue.

Didn't help that those deep, teal blue eyes of his stayed locked on hers, instead of doing that scan-her-body-to-check-out-the-goods thing she was used to from the few blind dates she'd been on.

This wasn't a date!

Right. She had to remember that.

"Hey, Tessa. You look great. Your wounds healing up okay?"

Oh dammit. Date or not, she was toast.

"They're fine. Thanks. Just a few bumps and scrapes."

His hand just barely ghosted over the middle of her back as he stepped to the side and pulled open the door for her. "Thanks for letting me pick the restaurant tonight. I don't get out to actual restaurants all that much but this is one I've always wanted to try. Have you eaten here before?"

"A few times." After they made their way to the first

open table and at least three workers said hello to her, she admitted quietly, "Okay, that's a lie. Most of the workers who answer the take-out line know me by voice."

That earned her a low, deep chuckle from him and she felt the air in her lungs getting lost on its way to her brain. Quickly, she flicked her menu up to avoid the possibility of conversation while her brain gasped for the return of oxygen for its malfunctioning neurons.

When the waiter came and addressed her by name, she avoided making direct eye contact with the smile begging to be let loose at the corner of Brian's mouth.

"I'm still looking," she fibbed quietly. "You can get his order first."

After he requested the *pollo carciofi* pasta, she finally put down the menu she'd only been pretending to read. "Could I just get a slice of Nonna's ricotta pie and a slice of the Tuscan spinach pie?"

When she saw Brian curiously reach for the menu again with a puzzled look, she stopped him and pointed at the chalkboard by the cash register. "Those are the dessert specials this week. I, errr, already ate dinner."

A mild look of exasperation overtook his features.

Thank goodness, they were back to their status quo.

"You told Skylar you weren't going to be hungry until seven."

"I'm usually not," she defended, picking up her water glass to take a parched sip. "But I seem to be able to eat hotdogs at any time of the day."

She crunched down on some ice during the awkward pause that followed.

"Do you always give responses that only make sense to you?"

She thought about that for a moment and replied in all seriousness, "More than I intend to, probably. But I also think you bring it out of me more than most for some reason."

His smile was back again. "Fair enough. Okay, so if I ask you to answer in the form of a complete short essay so I'll fully understand you, could you tell me what's with the whole eating a hotdog before meeting me for dinner thing?"

Now she was smiling along with him. He was so darn easy to like, and surprisingly patient considering how easily she seemed to bug the crap out of him.

"Sometimes I hang out at the lumberyard where my dad used to work so I can watch the sunset from the top of the lumber stacks. And when I do, I always drop off a hotdog for my dad's old boss, Frank. He doesn't know that it's actually a low-cal, healthy mostly-veggie dog, which is why he always lights up like a kid on Halloween when I bring it over. Which is why I try and go pretty regularly. And I dunno, I just always automatically bring one for myself too. To keep the tradition alive, I guess."

She'd noticed Brian's eyes darken with sympathy when she first mentioned her dad in the past tense, and she mentally prepared herself for the question.

"So did your sister inherit her HD gene from your dad?"

"Yes. His was adult-onset obviously, but Willow's JHD symptoms started when she was in middle school. Maybe that's why I'm especially meddlesome in Skylar's case. Sorry." And she was, really.

Since the concession seemed to earn her some respect points from him, she opted for full disclosure. "To be clear though, I'm just sorry you're upset, not sorry that I'm answering all her questions."

He frowned. "Just when we were starting to get along."

They quieted as their food arrived, both leaving their plates untouched in an unspoken agreement that they'd get this hammered out first.

The moment the waiter left, Tessa had no problem starting them off. "Abby mentioned you were thinking of doing the testing last year. Why'd you change your mind?"

"Skylar had been showing some symptoms that we thought could be JHD then. *Symptomatic* genetic testing, the doctors and I were on board with. But now that she's been symptom-free for months, we've decided against it."

"Exactly. *She* didn't decide. You all did."

"She's not old enough to make this decision. I've read the studies; the youngest age they typically allow a minor to make this decision is fifteen, if that. She's just barely thirteen, way too young, too emotionally ill-equipped."

"Brian, Skylar has questions that need to get answered."

"By me, or her doctors. Not by you—no offense—or some random websites."

"At least the websites I directed her to were reliable, accurate, and just as importantly, non-persuasive. You're fooling yourself if you think she hasn't been reading up on every single thing about HD and JHD she's been able to find on the internet."

That made him pause with what looked like a flash of pained panic before he maintained, "You still had no right to be advising her about genetic testing behind my back, Tessa."

Okay, she'd give him that. "You're right. While I think it's important for Skylar to have someone to talk to and ask questions of beyond her current bubble, it was irresponsible of me not to have checked to be sure that you were at least aware of the situation. I know you're going through this as much as she is."

"Now that's just unfair," he sighed, leaning back and breaking into one of the dinner rolls at the table. "If you're going to be logical and respectful for a shocking first, I don't know how I can keep arguing with you."

She chuckled. "I have my moments." Seeing the worry still hiding behind his banter, she reassured him, "I swear, I'm just listening and answering questions. I'm not advising her in any way. I would never steer her in a direction that would be harmful to her, and I think you know that."

The stubborn man offered no more than an acquiescent half-nod.

"Are you going to fight me on this the entire time?" she asked, trying to hide the smile in her voice. Usually, confrontation was not her thing, but for some reason, the prospect of continuing to face off with Brian sounded *fun*.

"Are you going to continue to be a pain in my ass by answering her questions, regardless of what I say?" he returned, his eyes crinkling at the corners.

"Yes."

"Then yes, I hereby reserve the right to be an obnoxiously overprotective dad about all of this whenever the mood strikes me."

"So, just to get this recorded on the minutes, basically, we've just agreed to keep doing things exactly as we've been doing them?"

Breaking out into an amused grin, he conceded, "Yes. Now let's eat before my food gets cold, and yours gets warm."

She grinned. Smart-ass.

Enjoying herself more than she'd intended to, more than it was probably advisable to, she grabbed her knife to cut each pie in half lengthwise before taking a bite of first the creamy ricotta pie, and then the spongy, almondy spinach pie.

"So tell me more about your dad," said Brian, between bites of his chicken and artichokes. "You mentioned a lumberyard. Was he in construction?"

"Yep. Right out of high school, all the way up until he first started showing signs of chorea spasms in his hands. That's when Frank hired him as the security guard for the lumber yard. The hours were perfect since he and I used to switch off taking care of Willow. And it was a way for him to stay close to the trade." She smiled softly. "Since Frank rents out construction equipment as well—mostly small excavators, tractors, and things—sometimes, dad would get to work the equipment to check them before and after rentals, or during maintenance. I saw him at it a few times when I went to drop off food for him. I used to love just watching him. It used to make him so happy. He didn't have a whole lot left to be happy for, so I will always be eternally grateful to Frank for that."

"Hence the hotdogs," editorialized Brian.

"That's right." She grinned in surprise. "I do believe the hotdog tradition started soon after that. But the lumber stacks at sunset was actually my dad's tradition. My dad used to take his break around sunset and go sit up on the tallest stack to just watch the view. Once, Willow and I went up there with him. Frank and the guys rigged one of the forklifts so my dad could help Willow up. I still remember how tickled she was to ride the forklift, and how much the three of us had laughed up there. The guys had to bring out the flood lamps to help us down since we'd stayed up there until well after dusk." Blinking herself back to the present, she felt the pain come as it always did at the memories. "Not long after she died, it was my dad who got the ride up the forklift to sit beside me." With a silent breath, she held back the tears she never ever allowed herself to shed. "And now it's just me up there. No forklift."

⁂

HE'D NEVER BEEN on this side before.

It was a startling revelation, really.

All these years, he'd always been on the receiving end of the 'I'm so sorrys.' Oh, he'd said his fair share before, meant every one. But not like this. Not for a pain right before his eyes that rivaled, if not eclipsed his own.

For the first time, he heard the 'I'm sorry' for the actual apology that it was. He wanted to apologize to her for not being able to ease her grief, apologize for not having the perfect thing to say that could make it all better again, apologize for the universe being the cruel and unyielding bastard it could be.

Brian couldn't imagine losing two loved ones that close together. By Connor's estimation, Tessa had been just twenty years old when her sister died, and a brand new adult with a lifetime of hurt already when her father died shortly after. Honestly, if he'd lost Beth at that age, it probably would've broken him. Losing a second loved one soon after would've been inconceivable.

"I'm so sorry, Tessa."

"I know," she said softly. "Me too."

It wasn't the standard response. Or even a logical one. In fact, it was one of those answers they'd talked about earlier, the ones that seemed to only make sense to her.

Except this one, he actually got.

They sat in a comfortable silence for a bit, finishing their meals. By the time he was done, he saw that she'd only managed to finish half her pies. *Lightweight*, he chuckled to himself. Skylar and Abby would each be on their second helpings by now if given half the chance—sugar junkies that they were.

"What are you smiling at?" she asked, eyes dancing in amusement. "No fair hoarding all the happy thoughts."

"I was just thinking that you need to train with Skylar and Abby. A few days with the sugar twins and you'll be able to whack those two pies and then some."

A surprised laugh tinkled out of her then. "You think I can't finish these pies?"

Christ, he loved that laugh.

"I could give the sugar twins a run for their money, thank you very much. Especially when it comes to pies. Seriously, give me a pie over cake and ice cream any day." Still chuckling to herself, she leaned over and slid the plates forward. "I was just saving the rest for you to try."

He wasn't at all prepared for the warm thump he felt in his chest.

"You are unlike anyone I've ever met," he told her, shaking his head. "You're always surprising me."

"Let me guess, you hate surprises," she teased.

He picked up his fork to take a chunk of the odd, green pie and then slid the rest back to her to finish. "Not so much anymore."

The brief moment they seemed to be having was pierced like a bubble at the sudden sound of a familiar musical medley he couldn't quite place.

"That's me." Tessa grabbed her phone, with its classic Rosie the Riveter *'We Can Do It!'* decal proudly displayed on its back. She furrowed her brow in non-recognition at the screen and then answered it anyway.

Her sad frown soon after, followed by a firm, "I'll be right there," instantly had him on alert.

Why he felt so overwhelmingly protective of a woman he barely knew, he had no idea. "Everything okay?"

"It will be. I'm afraid I have to cut our dinner short. Normally I wouldn't ask, but do you think you can follow me back to my place and then drive me over to Cactus Creek?"

"Now?" Brian checked his watch. Damn, they'd been talking for hours. "Most everything there will be closing by midnight."

"I know but a friend of mine is sloshed drunk at a bar and I need to drive him home." She headed quickly out to the parking lot. "If you can't, it's no big deal. I can call a cab to meet me at my apartment." She was already pulling out her cell phone.

And that bugged him to no end.

"No, it's alright. I'll take you. Skylar is at a sleepover so I'm free. Let me help." His eyebrows shot up when he saw her climb into an old grandpa Rambler wagon...which had what sounded like a hemi engine.

Honestly, the woman just didn't have a normal bone in her body.

"Thanks, Brian. Okay, just follow me."

A frighteningly quick minute later—speed limits were apparently a laughable suggestion and yellow lights a dare for Tessa—she was parked and climbing into Brian's SUV. "Do you know the way to *One-Eyed Snake*?"

"The biker bar?" Geez, never a dull moment.

"Yup. My friend Isaac does this sometimes, and since I programmed my number into his cell phone under the name '*If I'm Drunk Off My Ass*,' if he's ever too drunk to drive, I occasionally get a call from a bartender to come get him."

"Is your friend an alcoholic?"

She shook her head sadly. "No, nothing like that. Not even close. He's just a good guy in a world of pain."

So a fellow kindred soul, then.

Brian took the highway exit towards Cactus Creek in silence. He was accustomed to the larger than life, bubbly Tessa. This quiet, sad side of her tugged at his heart. While also captivating him all the more.

"Isaac and I met in a grief group," she revealed in the silence. "He lost his younger brother around when I lost Willow. We became friends right off the bat. We're not the talk-all-the-time sort of friends like you and Abby are, but if ever I get a call from a bartender, I always go running."

Somehow, that didn't surprise him.

They pulled into the parking lot of the rustic bar and she hopped out before he even shifted into park. "I got it from here, Brian. Thanks for driving me. I'll call you sometime this week so we can talk about the whole HD testing thing some more. Sorry we didn't get to—" She frowned and backed up when he got out of the car. "What are you doing? You can head home. I promise, I've got it from here."

Yeah, like he was really going to let her go into a biker bar alone. The fact that she looked so damned surprised that he wasn't leaving her there shot another dart into his chest. "Come on, let's go get your friend."

With a resigned shrug, she turned and just headed on in. As if her serene smile, Smurfs t-shirt, and frayed denim skirt over backless sneakers weren't the most misplaced thing in the joint.

She was driving him nuts.

As she headed for the bar, the tatted-up bartender looked up, one eyebrow raised. "I take it you're '*If I'm Drunk Off My*

Ass?'" His glance swept over her up and down, and Brian felt his hackles rise.

"Damn, you *are* as sweet and delicate as you sounded on the phone. I was hoping, but at the same time not. You do know that Isaac rode his Harley down here, right?"

"The V-Rod is his usual bar-going ride of choice," she replied matter-of-factly, scanning the room for her friend and finding him in the corner, all but passed out.

"Alright," said the bartender, shaking his head and handing her Isaac's phone, but holding onto his keys. "I don't normally allow this but I can lock his bike up in the back for you until tomorrow afternoon."

She gave him a surprised smile—damn near lighting up the whole room in the process—and scooped Isaac's keys from his hands. "Thank you but I got this. I can ride. Plus, that's Isaac's brother's bike. I can't let it out of my sight."

A measured pause, and then, "Is that the brother he's been talking about all night?"

She nodded.

The bartender gave a quiet look of sympathy. "Okay then. You sure you can handle it? That's a lot of bike."

Pulling out a twenty, she slid it over to him. "I'm fine. Thanks for calling me."

"I already charged the standard tip for his drinks on his card, hon. You can put your money away."

With a determined stare, she walked over and shoved the bill at him. "This tip is my ridiculously small way of saying thanks. Not every bartender would take the time to go through a drunk customer's phone or find out which bike is his. You did. You didn't just boot his ass into a cab and leave his bike out in front to get stolen. You genuinely care. I heard it when you called and I'm looking at it now. You're a good bartender and an even better guy. Take the tip or not, your choice." She shrugged. "I'm just going to leave it on the counter regardless."

Then she just up and walked away.

Holy shit. The little hellion was more potent than a shot of illegal moonshine.

And evidently, he wasn't the only one who thought so.

Reaching over to pocket the twenty, the bartender couldn't take his eyes of Tessa. "Sugar, if your boyfriend wasn't looking ready to tackle me, I'd be embarrassing myself in front of all my regulars right now begging you for your number."

Tessa laughed. That damn, captivating laugh that had a half dozen heads at the bar turning her way. "That's my friend Brian. He's not my boyfriend."

An amused chuckle rang out from behind the bar. "Tell *him* that."

Smart bartender.

Tessa tossed them both a puzzled look and went over to retrieve her friend—a guy that could've passed as a bouncer for this very bar. Even though he was too drunk to stay on his feet without swaying, the second he saw Brian, the man's frame went stiff, fists at the ready as he exchanged a few hushed words with Tessa. One drunkenly blinking eye on Brian the entire time.

With an arm wrapped around his waist, Tessa walked Isaac out of the bar, exchanging mollifying introductions as she walked Isaac over to the row of bikes out front. It wasn't until Tessa mentioned him being Connor's brother—and just a friend she'd spent the night discussing HD testing with—that Isaac eased off with the suspicious glaring.

Seemed like the need to protect her wasn't his

compulsion alone.

Brian watched then as Isaac barely managed to throw his leg over his Harley.

"Tessa, you can't be serious. The guy is too drunk to sit up, let alone hold on to you. He'll take you both down if you try and ride double with him."

The corner of her lip rose up. "Are you offering to ride double with him instead?"

He scowled at her. "I'm being serious. Were you telling the bartender the truth? Do you really know how to even ride this thing?"

"Yes. I took lessons years ago." She met his eyes quietly. "It was one of the things Willow always wanted to do."

He cataloged that info to read more into later. "Still, this is dangerous and you know it." He helped Isaac off the bike. "C'mon, let's get him in the SUV. Then you drive and I'll follow you on the bike."

She pulled back. "Have you ridden a Harley V-Rod before?"

Admittedly, no. But he'd driven a few dirt bikes when he was younger and the occasional buddy's motorcycle in college. "It can't be that different a ride."

With a fierce headshake, she clutched Isaac's keys tighter. "Sorry, no can do. I'm not letting you near the bike."

Annoyed, he bit back. "I'm not going to wreck it."

Surprised, she looked up. "I was worried about you hurting yourself. But yes, now that you mention it, I can't let anything happen to the bike either. But I will take you up on the offer of putting Isaac in the SUV. It'll save me from using his belt to buckle his arms around me like last time."

He came to a stuttering halt. "You did *what* last time? Tessa, the guy's got a hundred pounds on you, easy."

"I didn't get on the freeway or anything," she defended, chin raised stubbornly. "Isaac has actually never come to this bar before. Normally, he sticks to bars in Mesa or Tempe. Since I don't exactly know where he lives, I usually just coast us over to get some coffee and food in him to sober him up enough to ride back to my place where he sleeps it off. And I go really slowly. You could call me Fred Flintstone by the way I ride."

Such an illogically weird reference, that, for some reason made him want to protect her even more.

"Fine. You ride the bike. But just because I'm morbidly curious to see if you can actually adhere to a speed limit. You go slow though, you hear? I'm talking granny-on-a-scooter slow. I'll be right behind you the entire time."

Smiling, she suddenly jumped up and kissed him on the cheek. Out of the clear blue sky.

"What was that for?" he asked gruffly, wanting seconds.

"Your alpha-protectiveness. It's growing on me. It's sweet."

Sweet? That was the last description he wanted to hear coming from her mouth. He didn't want Tessa to think of him as the sweet guy she could just give an innocent peck on the cheek to.

He wanted more.

"She meant it as a compliment," came the slurred commentary from his backseat.

Brian glanced up in the rearview mirror.

Isaac blinked at him slowly. "Tessa. She hasn't had sweet guys in her life. It's actually a hell of a compliment."

And then he passed out again.

Huh. Brian processed that drunken revelation later while half-dragging Isaac up to Tessa's little one-bedroom apartment. After dropping him onto her living room couch, Brian motioned for Tessa to follow him back outside.

"Why don't I stay over tonight too?" he offered. "Just give me a spare pillow; I'm fine sleeping on the ground. Better to be safe than sorry. I mean I know he's crashed here before, but let's face it, he's really drunk and he's a guy."

She gave him a reassuring headshake. "You don't have to worry about Isaac. He wouldn't try anything, trust me. He's in love with a woman from his past. Random flings are the only thing he's open to while he waits on her. And that's just never going to happen with us."

No, just as he'd thought. A girl like Tessa wouldn't be open to just a fling.

Then again, for a girl like Tessa, Brian wasn't sure he'd be open to just a fling either.

"Isaac and I have been friends too long," she continued. "And since I don't have a whole lot of friends, I make it a point not to fling or get flung by one."

Funny, Brian would think a woman as full of life as Tessa would have a ton of friends.

"I guess you could say we're more like each other's emergency brake if we ever find ourselves sliding backward down a hill." She shrugged. "No muss, no fuss. We just know to screech the other to a halt since we already know exactly what the other is going through."

Been there. Never really had that.

"So he's in your phone directory too?" he asked, envious over that somehow. He wanted to know Tessa as fully as Isaac seemed to. Though even then, she was so fiercely independent, he wondered how fully anyone truly knew her.

"Yeah, but not as a drunk-in-the-bar contact. Just as Isaac. I guess I've never used the emergency brake 'advanced feature' of our friendship."

Then what's kept her from crashing all these years?

"Hand me your phone," he said gently.

Giving him a look, she passed it over, a faint smile on her lips as she watched him type something into her phone. When his phone rang a moment later, he disconnected her end and gave it back to her while quickly typing in something on his own phone.

He watched her curiously scroll through her friend directory—a short scroll—and smile wider when she saw the new name he'd put in her contacts list. "*'If I Just Did Something Insane,*'" she read aloud with a chuckle. Then she looked up and read his screen, which he was displaying with the contacts entry he put for her phone number, "*Caution--Crazy Woman.*"

She laughed. "Nice."

"Oh, and I put my cell phone number in there instead of my landline because I don't want to be getting what's sure to be daily calls of insane reportings on my home phone."

She whacked him in the gut in relaxed humor. He caught her hand and tugged her closer, enjoying the return of her smile with a long lost ease that was as welcome as it was confusing, as turbulent as it was comfortable.

Smoothing her hair back, he gave her a soft kiss on the cheek. "Don't do this by yourself anymore, sweetheart. If you'll let me—and I really hope you do—I'll be your emergency brake from now on. Whenever, wherever."

He climbed in his SUV and started it up, rolling down the window before he shifted into gear. "And could you do me one huge favor?" he called out.

She smiled hesitantly. "Sure."

"Lock your bedroom door tonight. I know he's your

friend and all, but the thought of him being just a few feet from you in bed is killing me...almost as much as it's killing me to think of you sleeping anywhere but my bed tonight."

At her quiet gasp, he just gazed at her for a parting second before saying softly, "Sweet dreams, Tessa. I had a great night."

CHAPTER FOUR

ALL WEEK, she'd thought about the feel of his lips on her skin...about being in his bed...about being in his bed while he did more than just kiss her cheek like a gentleman.

Today alone, she'd been so hot and bothered by all the possibilities, she'd had to restart the prep on three dishes for tonight's catering event.

She had it bad.

"Hey Tessa. Sorry we're a little late."

At the sound of Connor's voice, Tessa glanced up and smiled.

"Hey guys. Are we late?"

At the sound of that second voice from the other entrance, Tessa's smile froze...and her heart rate went from a trot to a gallop. *What the heck is Brian doing here?*

Funny how the two brothers sounded so alike and yet Brian's voice was the one that had her nearly forgetting why she was holding a tasting fork in each hand. She turned just in time to see Connor look over at his brother in surprise.

"Hey, man. I didn't know you were helping Tessa out tonight, too."

Neither did I.

Even though Brian's eyes shifted over to address Connor,

Tessa could still feel his attention on her.

Okay, seriously, why were her hands still holding two folks midair?

Right, tasting. While the guys chatted, she awkwardly jammed a fork in both of their directions. "Want a taste?" she offered lamely, blushing when she saw the sizzling hot awareness in Brian's eyes dial up to scorching as he answered her silently.

Yes.

Tessa quickly spun back around to the stove, their murmured compliments over the food barely audible over the blood pounding in her ears.

Hearing the loud, jovial sounds of Abby and Skylar gabbing away as they entered the ballroom kitchen was her only saving grace. Grabbing two more tasting forks, she took a sample of two different entrées and greeted them without missing a beat. "Hi Abby. Hey Skylar. Burgundy-braised pork loins in this one, and the other is stuffed beef tenderloin."

"Yum," praised Skylar. "Crazy good stuffing."

"This pork is like butter," chimed in Abby. "You seriously need to teach me how to make this glaze. I'd eat it by the bowl-full."

Finally feeling her nerves settle, Tessa smiled. "Oh good. I was pretty sure I didn't screw it up, but I don't usually handle much more than the prep and finish for the non-dessert dishes. I mean I've helped Lana do individual steps of almost all the dishes a bunch of times, but I'm definitely a better baker than I am a cook." She mentally stuck a tasting fork into her brain to stop her rambling. "Anyway, thank you guys again for swooping in to help at the last minute. This is the first time Lana has been sick during an event."

Tessa knew she'd only managed to turn it down from a

ramble to a babble but she was downright frazzled. And it wasn't just because of Brian's nerve-wracking presence. It was because of the entire event itself.

Her ten-year high school reunion.

Sort of.

To avoid that train wreck of a reminder altogether, she just switched her brain to autopilot. She could do this. This was just like any event. And Brian was no different than the other helpers they sometimes booked for bigger events.

Riiight.

She plastered on a big smile and dove in feet first.

"Connor, Abby, could you two set up the dessert station for me? I have a photo of the standard set-up we use over by the serving carts. There will be five trays of desserts so if you could just space it accordingly, that would be awesome."

"No problem." Abby went over to grab the photo and quickly ushered Connor out the door.

Grabbing two pitchers, Tessa handed them over to Skylar. "I've left all the chafers—those metal trays that keep the food warm—at the serving stations out in the ballroom. Do you think you and your dad could take these pitchers and fill each of the pans out there with about an inch of water and then get the fire going on them? I'll have all food ready to go out when the water gets hot enough."

"Sure." Skylar headed over to the sinks at the other end of the kitchen to fill the pitchers.

Then at the drop of a footstep, the kitchen suddenly felt no bigger than a broom closet.

Tessa didn't even have to look up to know that Brian was now standing beside her.

"I didn't get a chance to say hi. I like the blue hair, by the way. Maybe even better than the pink and purple." He placed a kiss on her cheek. The other cheek, this time.

Not that she was keeping track or anything.

"Hey, Tessa did you want us to—" Connor's voice halted mid-sentence and disappeared as he got jerked by the collar right back out of the doorway.

Tessa blushed. "I take it Abby was the one that asked you to come help?"

"Yep. In what was the most obvious set-up of all set-ups."

Her cheeks were going to burst in flames at this rate.

And feeling the back of his fingers brush over her heated skin didn't help the cause one bit.

"Brian, I have no idea why she did that. I swear, I haven't even told her we went to dinner last week."

He grabbed the candle lighter and volleyed back, "Who said the set-up was on your behalf?" before heading over to help Skylar carry out the pitchers.

∽∂∽

CONNOR CORNERED ABBY at the far end of the buffet station, out of earshot from Skylar. "Is someone sticking her cute little nose in where it doesn't belong?"

His impish wife looked up and batted her lashes at him. "What do you mean? Tessa needed the help. And when I heard how big the event was, I figured it'd be best to call Brian."

Uh huh. "For an event involving *cooking*?"

"Whiiich is why I also called in Skylar."

Connor chuckled. "So Brian talked to you about Tessa, huh?"

In an instant, her grin vanished and turned into a piqued

pout. "Wait, Brian's been mentioning Tessa to you?"

Shit. Major guy-code violation. "No," he backpedaled. "Not *specifically*..."

"You're lying!" It was an indignant, hands-on-hips huff. Cute as hell.

"Possibly," he fessed up, smiling as he offered graciously, "Of course I might know for sure if I'm lying or not if you tell me what Tessa's been telling you about Brian."

Brian and Tessa were so going to kick their asses for this.

Abby maintained military silence for all of three seconds before her curiosity got the better of her. "Okay, Tessa hasn't been talking to me about Brian per se. But she did comment out of the blue once that Brian is really alpha intense."

He blinked. "And you're sure she was talking about Brian *Sullivan*?" His brain couldn't even find a long enough thread to link the two descriptors to his brother.

Bobbing her head excitedly, she was practically giddy. "That's why I invited him tonight."

Connor chuckled. "Well, this is going to be interesting."

※

THIS WAS THE FIRST TIME since Connor's wedding that Brian was seeing Tessa all buttoned up in that white catering uniform. He much preferred seeing her in her off-the-wall novelty tees she always paired with a denim or flowing gypsy skirt. She looked...more *her* that way.

And he was really starting to like her being her.

He'd known this was a set-up from the first thirty seconds of Abby's call a half hour ago, but he went along with it anyway because he'd wanted to see Tessa.

He was starting to get addicted to the woman.

After finishing up getting all the warming stations going on the buffet line, he sent Skylar to help Abby and Connor finish up at the dessert table and headed back down the corridor to the kitchen to see what else Tessa needed done.

"I'm telling you guys, that's her. You can't tell because she's all covered up, but that's definitely that chick we almost pulled a train on out at the lakes our sophomore year."

Brian rolled his eyes in disgust as he neared the group of guys standing out in the hallway near the restrooms. Those were the very guys he'd avoided in high school. Pathetic that some of them just never seemed to grow out of it.

"I know that night was her first time but she would've been all over you guys too if those other girls hadn't thrown up all over the place and killed the mood for everybody. The girl was a freak—still is, I bet. Look at that club skank hair with the blue streaks. She's probably wearing something slutty right now under that chef coat."

Brian saw red.

Murderous, bloodthirsty anger pumped through his system, all rational thought gone. Those assholes were talking about Tessa.

And he was going to make them pay.

"Brian, *no.*"

The horrified voice sounded so far away, but somehow it pierced through the haze of rage tunneling out his vision, filling his veins with adrenaline.

Not enough to stop him though.

That's when Connor entered his narrowed field of vision and shoved him back against the wall. "Brian, calm down."

He couldn't even begin to form words. The three dead men walking had turned around to see what the commotion was, and he was itching for them to come over and find out.

Tessa clamped her hands down on his forearm. "Just let it go, Brian. That guy's a dick, not worth your time or anger."

"*What'd you just call me, bitch?*"

"For crissakes, the dumbass has a death wish," muttered Connor as he shoved his forearm up against Brian's throat to keep him pinned against the wall. "While I'd love nothing more than for you to pound the shit out of him, I'm telling you, just walk away."

But he didn't have to go anywhere at all, because Dumb, Dumber, and Dumbest were so conveniently bringing the fight to him.

"Gavin, dude. Enough. Come on, let's just go back in to the party."

Well, at least one of them had at least part of a brain.

'Gavin,' who was clearly drunk and maybe even a little high, elbowed his friends back and kept right on coming, glassy eyes, prickish strut and all.

"*Do we have a problem out here, gentleman?*" The uniformed officer that was serving as security for the event stepped into the hallway, with the people from the reception table at the front trailing close behind.

Gavin turned around and squinted at the approaching officer for a second before chortling loudly, "Trey? Is that you, man? It's me, Gavin. You played football with my brother. Dude, you're a legend!"

Trey didn't even dignify that with a blink. "I asked you folks a question. Is there a problem here?"

Tessa rushed forward. "No problem, officer. My team and I are just trying to get the food out for the reunion—"

"No, no, we do have a problem, Trey," interrupted Gavin. "Because here I was just minding my own business, trying to catch up with my high school buddies, and then out of nowhere, I got verbally assaulted by this skanky high school dropout here."

"*You fucking*—" It took both Trey and Connor to slam Brian back against the wall. And this time, it was the fridge-sized cop and his massive forearm that was nearly cutting off his air supply. "Don't do it, man. I don't want to have to arrest you."

Trey fired a withering cop-stare over at Gavin. "I suggest you return to the ballroom and not bother this young lady any more. If I find you so much as talking to her again, I'll be personally seeing to it that she files a harassment charge against you."

Gavin looked around at all the eyes glaring at him with varying degrees of repugnance and wrath. "Whatever. I'm going back to the party," he shot out with a weaselly grunt. He turned around in a complete, drunken circle then, looking for his two sidekicks.

They were nowhere to be found.

Looking far less cocky now, Gavin tossed Tessa one last hateful look and then slinked off around the corner.

Trey turned to Brian. "Sorry man, but since you're not a guest, and there were specific complaints from the workers here about you, I'm going to have to ask you to leave as well."

Brian growled. "I'm not leaving Tessa alone here with that asshole."

A calm, cultured voice rang out from behind them. "Don't worry, my wife and I will stay with Tessa tonight."

⊸≫⊶

TESSA TURNED to look at the distinguished man walking toward them with the gorgeous redhead on his arm.

"Tessa, you probably don't even know who I am—"

"James," she said with a smile. "Of course I know who you are. We had geometry class together."

A surprised grin transformed his face, made him look even more like the boy who always used to help her with her classwork. "Yes. I can't believe you remember me. We only had one class together."

"A class I would've failed had it not been for you." She reached out to shake his hand and then his wife's.

"Well, like I said, Marcy and I will be happy to help out," repeated James. He looked over at Brian. "Tessa won't even have to leave the kitchen at all. We'll handle everything out in the ballroom."

Tessa shook her head, instantly rejecting the generous offer. "No, don't be silly. You're guests tonight. I can handle the rest on my own, really. Everyone can just head home and head back to the party. There's not all that much left for me to do."

Marcy stepped forward. "Our minds are already made up. In fact, we'll probably even run a little wager on who can run the smoothest buffet line. Even at the restaurant where we work, we're terribly competitive."

"Which restaurant?" asked Connor. "Because you two look really familiar."

"James and I are both line chefs at *Le Mille Feuille*."

One of the most elite five-star restaurants in Arizona.

"Holy shit." The commentary was a soft murmur from behind Connor.

"Skylar, language!" scolded Abby, though her expression mirrored the sentiment.

When Tessa looked over and saw Skylar sliding worried looks over at her dad, a kaleidoscope of clips from the last ten minutes flooded Tessa's brain all at once, all the awful things Gavin had said…things Skylar had undoubtedly heard, things Brian had been willing to assault another man over.

The room spun.

"Tessa?" Brian pushed past everyone and gripped her elbow, easing her away from the group and toward the open side door so she could get some air. "You okay, sweetheart?"

The intense concern she saw in his eyes humbled her. "Brian, thank you for defending me back there but I'll be okay. Why don't you go on and take Skylar home. Please. She shouldn't be around this."

And you shouldn't be risking jail time to defend someone like me.

He reached down to pry her clenched fists open and ordered gently, "You make sure to stay in the kitchen the entire night." Turning to look at Officer Trey, the two exchanged one of those top secret 'guy' head nods before he added, "And don't go out to your car alone. Have either James or Officer Trey keep you company while you load everything back up."

Out of the corner of her eye, she saw James and Marcy off to the side nodding in agreement.

"Promise me, Tessa." It was that alpha-protective rasp, laden with worry.

She stared at him for a moment and shook her head lightly. At his fierce scowl in response, she quickly explained, "No, I wasn't saying no. I was just…amazed, I guess. I'm not used to people worrying about me, being protective over me."

He smoothed his thumb over the nail marks she'd dug into her own palms. "Get used to it."

Her breathing stopped in her lungs altogether.

"Last thing. Connor said you live in Mesa, not far from

me. After you're done packing up, I want you to come over for a bit. I'll text you the address. I want to make certain that no one follows you home without you knowing. I need to see for myself that you're safe."

"Brian, you're being paranoid—"

"I saw the way that guy looked at you, Tessa. And after a night of drunken glory day reminiscing with the rest of his dumbass friends, who knows what he'll do. Swear to me you'll come straight over to my house after finishing up here."

His quiet gaze, almost raw in its intensity, fell down to her lips in the sweetest promise of a kiss she'd ever received. "Promise me, Tessa."

Touched beyond words, she nodded. "I promise. I'll be there by ten at the latest."

CHAPTER FIVE

SHE GOT THERE at 9:30.

Which brought an official end to his checking-the-clock-every-ten-minutes fun.

Brian had the front door open and the interrogation started before she even hit the doorbell. "Are you okay? Did that guy harass you any more tonight?"

Jesus, the thought of her there without him had clawed at his insides all night. He knew Tessa had been right about his taking Skylar home, but every male cell in his body had fought him on it, demanded he stay there and protect her.

His woman.

The thought blindsided him.

"Gavin didn't come near me for the rest of the night," she answered, breaking into his thoughts. "I actually had a pretty okay night. James and his wife are probably one of the most interesting couples I've ever met. And they made certain I never had to leave the kitchen the entire time. They hovered over me all night. Officer Trey, too. He wouldn't even let me go to the restroom unescorted." The look of baffled wonder in her expression when she talked about the couple and the officer tugged at his heart. She really wasn't used to anyone taking care of her, that much was clear.

And that just made all his alpha protective instincts kick up even more. He scanned the street to make sure she hadn't been followed and pulled the door wider to let her in.

"No, that's okay. It's late," she declined, half-turning to go. "I just came by to say thanks again. Maybe we can go out sometime to—"

He caught her elbow to keep her from walking back to her car. "Hang out for a bit. One beer to take the edge off."

Though he was working damn hard at it, he couldn't smooth out the rough gravel in his voice. The idea of her going back to her apartment alone tonight after how broken she'd looked earlier...

"I also have pizza. And ice cream," he attempted again, willing her to stay.

Her lips curved up at the corners. "Can we make beer floats?"

He almost laughed then. She was always saying and doing the completely unexpected. "Sure." He stepped back so she could walk in, and he had to forcibly order himself to stop holding on to her arm as if she were going to cut and run. "I have chocolate syrup and whipped cream too if you want."

Damn.

Her eyes widened and her step faltered just a bit.

One look at the color rising in her cheeks and he knew she'd been thinking the same thing he'd been. Well...maybe not the *same* thing. He was pretty sure that his thoughts starring her naked after he'd licked chocolate syrup and whipped cream from her body wasn't exactly what was running through her mind.

But then he saw those witchy bedroom eyes of hers dip down to the front of his jeans—for just a fraction of a second—and he nearly groaned out loud.

Yeah, okay, so maybe what she was thinking was better.

Her flushed cheeks went higher up the color scale and she spun around quickly to head for the kitchen. "I'm going to raid your fridge to get started."

It took him a while, but eventually he remembered his brain needed oxygen to survive. So he started working on that while heading over to the cupboard for the thick glass mugs Skylar had insisted he buy for her movie night cream soda floats.

"There's some Guinness way in the back," he offered helpfully. "Not sure how the other beer will taste in a float."

Her voice drifted out from depths of the fridge, sounding pleasantly surprised. "For a guy who looks like he could bench press a brontosaurus, you're awfully familiar with beer float basics." She pulled out two bottles of Guinness with a look of triumph. "It's actually kind of a turn-on," she teased.

He had a feeling she was simply talking without a filter again rather than flirting, so he kept it tame. Relatively. "While I definitely like the idea of turning you on, I can't take the credit for this one. My friend Danni owns a brewpub in Cactus Creek and she puts beer in absolutely everything. She talked my ear off about beer floats one day before adding it to her menu."

"Get out, are you talking about *Ocotillos*? I love that place."

Not surprising. It was unique and outside-the-box, very much like Tessa. "Well then we have to go hang out there sometime. I'm sure Danni would love to pick your brain on how she can bake more beer into her desserts."

"That sounds like fun."

The return of her smile was a welcome sight. He liked being responsible for that smile. He wanted to *keep* being responsible for that smile as much as possible.

Grabbing the mugs, she glanced down the hall. "Should we make a cream soda float for Skylar? Or is she asleep already?"

"She's out like a light. Lately she's been doing that a lot. Unless she's hanging out with her best friend, I can barely keep her awake long enough to let her rot her brain on video games and stuff like a normal kid. Can't remember the last time she's stayed awake through a movie."

"Have her doctors ruled that out as a symptom?" asked Tessa quietly.

Seeing her worried expression, he went with the whole truth, not the watered down version he usually gave Connor. "For now. Though we are adding it to the equation. But because she isn't exhibiting any other social or psychological symptoms, we're calling it basic adolescent fatigue. But monitoring it."

"Good, I'm glad. She's a good kid. You've done a great job raising her."

"Thanks. It's been a team effort." Grabbing a handful of napkins along with some straws and spoons, he joined her and the two huge beer floats waiting for him at the dining table. He noticed she'd opted not to use the chocolate syrup or the whipped cream.

Probably for the best.

"Skylar really likes you," he added. "Which says a lot." He lifted his spoon to clink hers in a toast before giving the foamy concoction a try. "She was pretty pissed off on your behalf tonight. I didn't realize it until Connor told me but while he was busy holding me back, Abby had to all but step on Skylar's feet to hold her back as well."

A small smile peeked through the cloud that had settled

over her face at the mention of the night's events. After taking a big sip of creamy beer, she said softly, "Brian, what that guy said earlier about my being a slutty high school dropout—"

She wouldn't meet his eyes, couldn't hide the shame in her voice, and that just made him want to hunt that asshole down all over again. "The guy's a jerk. He—"

"—wasn't lying." Her voice shrunk smaller still. "Well, the slutty part is a gross exaggeration, but the dropout part is true. I dropped out after my sophomore year. But I got my GED right away at a job that was practically full-time…" She paused the rush of words when his hand touched her forearm.

"Hey, slow down. I figured that was the case. From what Connor tells me, all you do is work. With all of your sister's hospital bills, it couldn't have been easy. I think it's noble that you dropped out to help with the bills—"

"That wasn't why I dropped out."

⁓

"I WAS THE BAD SEED."

Tessa's stomach pitched as she forced the words out. The irony of that particular statement had always been a bitter pill to swallow.

"Willow was the perfect daughter. She was kind and sweet, beautiful and talented, and just…perfect. In every way. She was my mom's pride and joy. Willow started playing the piano when she was four and she was a natural. My mom found her a piano teacher who was a former child prodigy, and after he took Willow under his wing, she became exceptional. By the time she was seven, she was composing her own music. I know there are more cases of that now, but back then, it was a really big deal. By the time she was ten, she was winning awards for her compositions."

Remembering just how extraordinary Willow had been filled Tessa with as much pride and happiness as it did pain. "But when Willow turned eleven, that's when she started developing symptoms. I'd been six or seven at the time, and while I don't remember exactly when or how I learned about Willow having JHD, I do remember my mom crumbling to pieces. She just disintegrated. She went from being the envied stage mom to the pitied mother fighting to keep her daughter alive—her perfect, talented daughter who was now unable to play the piano, unable to go to school, unable to do day-to-day functions."

Tessa dragged in a breath, swallowing the lump in her throat she always got when she was hit with the fleeting memories of her sister playing the piano. The small, disjointed snippets recorded in her mind were the only things left of her sister's music, since her mother had taken a drunken hammer to every homemade video of Willow's concerts. Tessa never told Willow that, never told her father either. Sometimes she wondered if even her mother remembered because it had been Tessa who'd cleaned up the carnage, bagged it up and threw it out—all of her sister's prize-winning memories.

"My mom wasn't a bad mom. She was actually very good at taking care of Willow, though she'd hated every second of it. She'd hated being terrified, hated having to provide CPR to her daughter until the paramedics arrived more times than she could count. She'd hated giving up her job, her friends, her whole life to take care of Willow every day. She'd hated the fact that the purpose of her days was solely about survival and not living."

"And most of all, she'd really, really hated being a mother...specifically our mother."

Brian took her hand. "Honey, I'm sure that wasn't true."

She shrugged sadly. "No, probably not. But she sure said it a lot to me. When she would remember me, that is. But I couldn't blame her. Look at all she had to do. She didn't have time to play with me, let alone remember my birthday or buy me Christmas presents. And with my dad working two jobs just to keep food on the table and medical bill collectors off of us month to month, I couldn't go whine to him about it either. Not when Willow was there being just the best big sister a girl could ask for, even while she was suffering through the most horrible disease."

Tessa remembered often how guilty she'd felt the few times she'd resented her sister. Moments of weakness, followed by several lifetimes of shame. For Tessa, there had been no one to take it all out on...so she'd taken it out on herself.

"From there, the start of my teen years was like a bad made-for-TV movie—hanging out with the wrong crowd, trying pot, skipping school, doing every stupid, self-destructive thing a kid could do...including having sex before I was ready."

When she felt Brian tense in remembered rage beside her, she just focused on keeping down the bile that rose up to her throat whenever she thought about that night.

"What Gavin said about pulling a train—that simply wasn't true. There was no way I would've done anything like what he described. That night at the lakes was my first time. I'd been drunk, and I'd been hurt...drunk mainly *because* I'd been hurting. But instead of getting the guy who waited for me outside of the church so he could give me a birthday cake with sixteen candles, I got the guy who took my virginity on top of an old blanket on the ground. The part that he did get right was when he said those two other girls at the party threw up all over the place…namely, on me."

Head hanging down in shame, she finished, "And for the memorable finale, I went home later to find that my sister had been taken to the ER that night and had almost died."

"My mom couldn't even look at me, couldn't understand why I was doing this *to her* when she was going through so much already. And to this day, I'll never forget hearing her say to my dad, 'Why couldn't it have been Tessa? Why did God have to punish *Willow* with JHD?'"

Vicious anger slashed across Brian's expression.

Tessa, meanwhile, just wrapped her arms around her middle, feeling the kick to the stomach those two shouted sentences had been, as if it had just happened yesterday.

"It's not like I haven't asked myself the same question. Willow had all the promise, all the perfection. And yet she was the one to get JHD. It wasn't fair."

Reaching up to wipe away the single, tear that had managed to break free and slide down her cheek, Brian whispered almost harshly, "It would've been equally unfair if you'd been the one with JHD, sweetheart."

Tessa laughed bitterly at that. "No. It wouldn't have been. And what's more, my mother would never have ended up the way she did if it had been me instead." An almost sympathetic sadness hit her as it always did when she remembered how broken her mom had become by then. "In that moment, then and there at the hospital after hearing her say that, I decided that my mother deserved the chance to be free. Free from the motherhood she'd come to hate so much, free from the husband she'd eventually have to watch suffer through adult-onset HD."

"…And free from me."

She met his eyes for the first time since starting the morbid replay of her childhood. "So *that* was why I dropped out. I got my GED the summer after my sophomore year, went to the bakery near our house and begged the woman who'd always been so kind to me and Willow to train and hire me. Between my dad and me, we made a plan to have Willow's care completely under control by the end of the summer. And by Labor Day, my mom was a free woman, living halfway across the country from us, blissfully carefree."

At his infuriated expression—yes, something like that would upset a wonderful parent like Brian—she added, "But it's okay. I made sure Willow and my dad were better off without her. I took care of them, did everything she only deigned to do, but better. I *loved* them and filled their lives with as much life as I could." She took in a deep, steadying breath. "And later, when my mom needed money to get back on her feet, I took care of her too. Just because she didn't want to be my mom, didn't mean I was going to stop being her daughter."

She had to look away. The sympathy in Brian's eyes was too much. Pity, she was used to, even disdain and recrimination like during high school. But genuine, more-feeling-than-thought sympathy...never.

He tipped her chin up gently but firmly and brought her gaze level with his.

"You, Tessa Daniels, are even more amazing than even I can believe."

WITHOUT ANOTHER THOUGHT, and no further notice, he hauled her into his arms and took possession of her lips in a deep, sinking kiss that had an uncontainable growl thrashing out of his chest. The woman wasn't just amazing, she was intoxicating.

She was *his*.

The feeling of finally having her in his arms filled him with a bone-deep comfort and reckless need all in one. Her lips parted for him and he tried, really he did, to gentle his kiss, to slow things down. But she was consuming him whole.

Control nearly shot, he pulled back a bit to simply stare at her as she unraveled in his arms. He watched her teeth bite into her lower lip, watched her eyes become drowsy with desire and darken to almost black as he skimmed up the hem of her shirt. Just a sliver of an inch. Just enough for his calloused fingers to feel the smooth silk of her back.

The tiny little gasp that escaped her was his undoing.

His lips couldn't help but fall back to claim hers again. Fully this time. With no restraint, no end in sight. Her every reaction was a revelation, her every open, honest response simply high-octane fuel that fed his arousal. He rubbed his fingers over the base of her spine slowly and drank in all the tiny sounds he was sure she didn't realize she was making. Her body softened against his then, sinking into him as if her every pleasure was his alone.

And he was lost.

She was burning alive under his touch and more than anything, more than his next breath, he wanted to drown in that fire, bring it to a full-blown inferno that consumed them both whole.

...But not tonight.

"Babe we can't," he somehow managed to punch out. Voice gravelly, he drew his hands back to safer territory and said roughly, "You're hurting and your emotions have gone through the wringer tonight. I can't take advantage of you like that."

And yet still, he couldn't bear to let her go completely.

"Then don't," she replied simply, arms twining around his shoulders. "Let me take advantage of you."

Jerking back to put some head-clearing distance between them was about as painful as ripping off his own skin.

"Sweetheart, why don't we just hang out tonight? We can sit and talk more about those dickheads we ran into tonight if it'll help. Or we could just watch a movie…anything you want to do."

He quickly snatched her wandering hands as they traveled down his lats and started tugging at the hem of his t-shirt.

"Anything except that," he groaned. "Work with me here, woman." Raggedly, he put his forehead against hers and counted to ten to try and find the tattered remains of his restraint.

The thought almost made him laugh. Who was he kidding? He had no restraint when it came to Tessa. By the fifth second, his lips had already found their way back to hers.

And goddammit if her whole body didn't just *tremble* right there in his arms.

She was just so mind-wreckingly responsive. As usual, without even trying, she was driving him batshit crazy.

Tapping into a reserve even he didn't know he had, he broke off the kiss and took another step away from her.

Then he watched in sad disbelief as her expression became completely shuttered a half an instant later—closing him out behind the walls of a now ten-story castle and a moat filled with fire-breathing piranhas.

The lightning quick response time of her defenses was a

punch to his gut, a tragic reminder of how much she'd been through, how hard she'd had to fight to not let it all destroy her.

"Look Brian, if you don't want to, you can just tell me you know. I just thought we had something and we could have a great night exploring it. But hey, I'm a big girl. You don't have to make excuses to let me down easy."

He gave her a look that said he wondered about her IQ before grabbing her hand and dragging it over the zipper of his jeans. "Does that feel like I *don't want to?*"

Her eyes widened, and her grip closed tight around him.

Bourbon-soaked shards of glass went hissing down his throat. "For chrissakes, *stop.*" The blood supply in his brain was dipping down to a dangerous low.

And the damn temptress was clearly all torn up about it.

He glared at the smile she was biting back. "I'm glad you find this so amusing."

"It's not amusement; it's relief. Here I was thinking it was just me getting affected with my perpetually wet panties around you and all."

A seriously pained groan escaped him then. "To preserve my sanity—and your panties—don't use the word wet in any more sentences tonight."

She sighed. "I really don't know why you're making such a big deal out of this. It's just sex. I'm not looking for anything serious. You heard Gavin earlier this evening. Being the 'good girl' was never exactly my thing." She brushed up against the hardening ridge tenting his jeans to drive home her point.

With a muttered curse, he clamped one arm around her waist and tangled his free hand in her hair. "Sweetheart, this thing between us *is* a big deal," he said roughly, tugging gently on her hair and nearly losing it when she arched her back in response. Her fitted tee was so paper-frickin'-thin. One sharp yank was all it'd take to rip it right down the middle.

Good lord, he needed to find some control.

"Whether this thing between us lasts one night or ten, when—and yes I said *when* we have sex—I'll make damn sure that every single second of it seeps into your bones, burns into your memory, and turns into a relentless craving that makes you forget all the assholes from your past." He ran his lips along the thrumming pulse at her throat.

"And if I'm really lucky, it'll also help ruin you for all other men completely."

CHAPTER SIX

TOO LATE. She was already completely, irreparably ruined. Addicted.

Hopeful.

The latter being the scariest part of it all.

Because for the first time in her adult life, she was actually hoping that there really was such a thing as a happily ever after for a girl like her...

And a nice guy who calls the very next day.

Because he did. Just to see how her day had been. A few days after that? Same thing. By the week's end, the only thing that had kept Tessa from thinking about Brian non-stop was the sheer volume of work she'd had.

She rarely left her weekly editor duties until Friday but it had been unavoidable this week. They were having an unusually busy spring season on the catering end of things with one corporate function every few days, not to mention all the grant deadlines and other projects that she was working on with Connor's pro bono team. She was just thankful she didn't have to worry about the summer edition of *AZ Hotspots* for another few weeks—there were just not enough hours in the day.

Halfway through checking next week's online layout and the selection of articles for *AZ Potluck*'s spotlight focus on cooking with spring veggies and fruits, Tessa almost hit the ceiling when her phone rang. It was her landline, and the jarring clang echoing in her apartment wasn't a sound she heard very often.

"Hello?"

"Do you have plans tonight?"

A warm buzz filled her veins. She wasn't sure why she liked the fact that he didn't bother to say who it was but she did. It was…intimate, somehow. And very Brian. "Depends. Are you planning on ruining me for all other men tonight?"

Silence.

She sat there and smiled, waiting him out.

"Would you come over if I said yes?" he rasped out, calling her bluff.

Two could play at that game. "Yes."

"Jesus Christ, woman."

She chuckled. For a first attempt at flirting, she'd say that was pretty successful. "I'm actually working tonight. Why? What's going on?"

"Just wanted to hang out with you if you were free," he replied, sounding disappointed. "The girls are having their sleepover here tonight, and normally I'd make them sloppy joes or have a Mexican night, but since the weather's warming up, they decided they wanted to camp out back instead. You sure you can't make it? We're doing our famous take-out smorgasbord. We each get to pick one or two of our favorite take-out items and we have ourselves a little buffet."

Tessa was tempted. "Lucky kids. I've always wanted to go camping."

His voice warmed. "Damn. I'd say we could pitch a tent as well but my yard's not that big. And I'm not entirely sure I'd be able to behave myself."

Wow. Clearly, he was much better at the flirting thing than she was; her mind was doing somersaults.

"We could go camping for real one of these weekends," he offered then, his voice smiling as he added, "I'd see to it that neither one of us would have to worry about behaving."

Now the silence was on her part.

"That was mean," she said when her vocal cords finally started working again.

Chuckling, he assured her, "Wasn't trying to be. I find you make it hard for me to think before talking."

Oh. Well then they were even. "I'll take a very eager rain check on the camping. Sadly, I've actually never even been on a vacation, let alone one in the woods. I usually just work all the time. Enter tonight as exhibit A."

"Yeah, Connor mentioned you're a workaholic. Say, why don't you bring your work here? I should probably do some grading anyhow. And the girls usually don't resurface until at least nine the next morning. You wouldn't even have to bring a take-out dis. We'll have plenty of food."

Geez, he was making it so hard to say no. The food part

yes, but also the part about their working alongside each other. It sounded so…nice.

"I don't know," she waffled. "This week has been so crazy with a mid-week catering event and two grant revisions for a new HD clinical trial we weren't prepared for. My to-do list for *AZ Potluck* alone will probably keep me chained to my desktop until at least eight maybe."

"So come over after. That's around when the girls eat on the weekends anyway. Say yes, Tessa. I like spending time with you. I've been thinking about you all week."

Definitely ruined for all other men.

"Okay, yes. And you can put me down for take-out veggie paella."

⁂

"I'LL CALL ABBY and ask her to stay here with you two," said Brian firmly, as he filled up his plate with food and took a seat at the table across from Tessa. "I have third quarter open house conferences until late that night. And since Becky's folks are going to be there too for Becky's classes, you girls would be unchaperoned until after nine o'clock." He shook his head. "No can do, Sky-bug."

Seeing his daughter wind up with what looked to be a hell of a pitch, he settled in for a fast one.

"Dad, I'm almost fourteen. I can totally stay home alone. Becky's older sister used to babysit Becky and her little brother when she was fourteen."

Becky echoed that last rebuttal point, her expression

serious, her fast-bobbing head silently cheering her friend on for all thirteen-year-old girls everywhere.

"During the day, sure," Brian volleyed back, glad that he'd done his research for this particular battle—the girls seemed to forget that parents actually talk to each other when their children are busy plotting. "But that was never at night. Again, sorry kiddo. Discussion closed. We can pick this argument up again when you actually are fourteen."

Game, set, match.

Skylar sighed in a you're-lucky-I-love-you way and the two girls grabbed their plates and headed out back to their fully stockpiled tent, Becky praising Skylar for being *so close* this time.

Tessa just chuckled, waiting until the girls slid the patio door shut before teasing, "Do you honestly believe you're going to suddenly be able to loosen those apron strings next year?"

He gave her a look that cried out *Judas*, and she chuckled even louder, miming the zipping of her mouth shut and throwing away the key.

"Ha!" he let out in disbelief. "If I thought that had any chance of working, I'd steal that invisible key and bury it in my pocket."

Brian watched as Tessa paused in surprise and then tipped her head back to laugh so hard she almost fell off her chair. He'd never seen her without those colorful weekly-changing streaks in her hair—without it, her ink-black hair framed her face with a softness that made her look more delicate, vulnerable. Infinitely more memorable.

And when she laughed. Jesus. The effect could stop traffic.

It didn't take much for her dainty fairy-like features—dark cat-like eyes, petal soft skin, and full, just-kissed lips that curved up at the corners even when she wasn't smiling—to become the picture of unabashed joy.

That's what it was. Joy. Her eyes would fill to the brim with the stuff, and transform into those—for lack of better description—'dancing rainbow eyes' that Beth used to always go gooey over whenever she'd see it happen on smiling, cherubic children. Shining with humor, arched like two little half-moons over high, laughing cheekbones, those eyes alone could make anyone in a fifty-yard vicinity smile.

A stark contrast to the week prior.

For days after that night, he hadn't been able to shake the image of her telling him about her heartbreaking past, her eyes brimming with tears she simply refused to shed, her broken-angel features almost haunting in its pain.

He stared at her in wonder. "Seriously, Tessa, how is it that you can still laugh like that?"

"Like what?" She blinked, little bursts of laughter still seeping into her voice.

"Like the universe hasn't taken everything out of you and crushed your spirit, like it hasn't squeezed the humor out of your soul with its selective brutality."

She looked startled for a moment, but then recovered with a slow nod. "Sometimes I forget you know exactly what that feels like." Shaking her head, she said softly, "For a while, I couldn't laugh. Especially after Willow died. It's not easy to keep laughing. You have to be open to surprises, work at not shutting yourself off to them. When you focus so much on surviving, nothing is a surprise because you've prepared yourself for everything. That's why nothing is funny anymore. You can't laugh if you don't let the unexpected sneak up on you and take you by surprise."

She gave him a determined look and stood up. "Here, try this—go over to that window and look outside. Mentally catalog everything you see."

He looked out at the pitch-black scenery on the other side of the glass. "Everything I see in the dark?"

"Just do it. There's enough street light. Be quiet and concentrate."

The woman was cute when she was being bossy.

A tiny bit curious over where this was going, he turned and did as he was instructed, staring off into the night and taking inventory of the neighbor's fence off to the right, the house with the weird rock garden out front, three SUVs... He heard her shuffling around behind him. "What are you doing back there?"

"Stop getting distracted. Keep going," she said sternly.

When she fell all but silent behind him, he focused back on the bizarre task at hand. Street curb, tree, fire hydrant...

"Okay, now turn around and tell me what you see."

He pivoted toward her and heard it before he saw it—the airy hiss that registered in his brain a split second too late.

Followed by an ice-cold splatter webbing over his face.

Gaping, he swiped a hand down his face to clear the stuff out of his eyes.

The woman had actually sprayed him with a can of whipped cream.

Tessa's jaw fell open and she backed up a step. "I swear, I didn't know it was going to do that. I was just aiming for your mouth."

With a slow, simmering smile, he wiped the rest of the cream off on the sleeve of his shirt as he stalked toward her. "You're so going to get it."

Her eyes flicked down to take in just how much white foam was now staining his partly rolled sleeves and her lips twitched in a flagrant lack of remorse.

Despite the fact that she was laughing at his expense, he smiled wider. Mostly because he'd just added that escaped grin to the tally of things he was going to collect on.

"Now, Brian. Let's be rational," she tried reasoning. "You can't blame me for that food canister malfunction."

Another tiny giggle.

Check.

The closer he got, the more he wondered why exactly she wasn't even trying to run—

He found out moments later when she launched the whipped cream toward the dining room and bolted in the opposite direction toward the sliding patio door.

Clever little prey. Too bad she put too much stock in the bottle of whipped cream.

He snagged her by the belt loops and crushed her body back against his. The sudden explosion of ear-singeing curse words at full soprano intermixed with those drunken fairy giggles of hers had a ball of laughter building in his chest.

Naturally, she followed that up with the last possible thing he expected.

Rather than attempt to escape, she instead spun around and grabbed the two sides of his half-buttoned flannel shirt—or as Skylar called it, his country music award outfit—and rammed her face into the opening. She smooshed her face against the plain black t-shirt he wore underneath, and wrapped the two flannel sides around her head like a protective bubble from any whipped cream retaliation. Her laughter continued, of course, buried though it was against his chest.

"*This* is your defense of choice?" He burst out laughing. "The ostrich-head-in-the-sand move?"

He took a few steps forward and cracked up harder when she shuffled back quickly to keep pace. He was certain if the girls were to happen upon them in the house now, hopped up on candy as he was sure they'd be, they'd freak out thinking they were seeing an ass-backward centaur.

Two muffled words vibrated against his sternum.

"What was that?" He grinned, deliberately mishearing her. "Was that an 'I'm sorry?'"

That smoked her out.

"I said, 'You're welcome,'" she flung out quickly before diving back in.

Not nearly quick enough, however.

An indignant cry pierced the air as he smeared a dollop of salvaged whipped cream down across her face.

"Thank you, sweetheart." He kissed her forehead between side-splitting chuckles. "That was the first belly-deep laugh I've had in years."

She gave him an adorably disgruntled pout, and used his shirt to wipe her face before eventually chuckling and smiling up at him from ear to ear. "You should laugh like that more." Her eyes twinkled with more of that infectious joy. "It sounds good on you."

SUDDENLY, SHE FELT his warm hand cup her cheek and slide along her jawline. Just a gentle, mild little caress to swipe away a smudge of whipped cream at the corner of her mouth. But for some reason, it inspired her tongue to flick out and curl around the pad of his thumb.

Oh my.

An intense fireball of hunger flashed, *burned* in his eyes and then without a sound, he pivoted, grabbed her hand ,and quickly towed her to his bedroom.

The door slammed shut behind him, cloaking them in darkness.

"You drive me crazy, you know that?"

God, his voice had dropped even lower, to a sexy thunder down under rumble.

"Crazy in a good way or a bad way?" she managed to ask

as her eyes adjusted to the lack of light.

"Both." He circled slowly around her as if she were a dangerous animal...he was getting ready to pounce on. "You have no filter whatsoever. Not with what you do or say, and especially not with how you react."

"That's not *my* fault. You can just point that finger at yourself, buddy," she grumbled back before snapping her mouth shut.

Alright, so maybe he was right about the filter thing.

"*What?*"

Man, if looks could strip. She'd never felt this naked before, this out of control. Inwardly, she sighed. The guy just brought out the uncivilized in her.

Oh well. She came this far—may as well see where this ride ends. "You heard me." Her chin came up defiantly. "I can't think when you talk in that ridiculously sexy voice. Or when your biceps suddenly double in size in the middle of even the simplest of tasks, like lifting a coffee mug. And don't get me started on your eyes. My god, I almost walked into a wall the last time you smiled and your eyes went from that soft ocean blue to deep turquoise. I mean who does that?!"

It was like she just couldn't stop talking.

When he came to a standstill and stared at her like she'd lost her mind, she huffed, "It's simply not reasonable to expect a girl to have any sort of filter with all the steamy-eyed, bicep-bulging, talking-like-a-wet-dream-voice-over madness going on!"

Silence.

Huh, so where might one *buy* one of these filters, she wondered.

With a quiet curse, he stomped toward her and picked her up by the waist, not even pausing in his stride as he kept right on walking to the bed. Well, if he going to take her for a ride...

She speared her hands into his thick, tousled waves and nearly purred with pleasure.

"Stop being so damn open," he rasped, sounding like a man about ready to do the unimaginable, his lips a whisper away from hers.

"Stop being so damn irresistible," she threw back, digging her heels into the carpet until his body ran flush into hers and bulldozed her straight back, flat onto the bed.

The air wedged in her throat as she watched the outline of his granite-etched jaw clench and release. He was so beautiful. *Oh to hell with it.* She wrapped her arms around his neck and touched her lips to his throat. The quiet male hiss she heard shot her attention down to the fact that he was more than a little happy to see her. Impressively so. And her sigh of pleasure against his throat served as a live current of electricity that she felt run through him...everywhere.

His hands slid into her hair and tilted her head back before he brought his lips crashing down onto hers.

"You're so mind-screwingly sexy," he muttered gruffly against her lips before his tongue made another sweeping raid in her mouth. "For chrissakes, I feel like I have zero control around you."

FOR ONCE, Tessa didn't have a snappy comeback for him. And despite his current state, which was anything but funny, Brian grinned over that as he flicked his tongue out to slide along the seam of her lips in triumph.

But then he nearly bit his own tongue off.

"I like making you lose control," she whispered, sliding a hand down past his waistband.

He jackknifed upright and flipped her onto the bed, pulling her hand up out of his boxer briefs to pin both of her wrists behind her back, wedged against the mattress.

She wriggled against him. "You're always holding my hands down. Don't tell me, you have a thing for bondage?" she teased as she tried to escape his grip.

When he couldn't stop his hips from bucking sharply against hers in response, she stilled and met his gaze. "Um...do you? Because if that's what you're into, we can uh—"

Keeping her wrists in place with one hand, he clapped the other over her mouth in exasperation. "Don't you *dare* finish that sentence."

Her body stopped squirming finally but there were still the equivalent of floating cartoon question marks in her eyes.

She was going to be the death of him.

"Have I fantasized about bondage?" he rumbled, his voice straining at the seams. "Of course. What guy wouldn't want a woman at his sexual mercy for a change?" He let out another silent oath when her eyes sparked with naked, hungry curiosity. "Do I want to try it with you? Probably, one day. It'd be hot as hell."

"And if you don't stop talking, that one day is going to be today—all your work deadlines be damned. So for the love of God, stop pushing me before you sentence us to an even longer bout of hot, hard, take-you-six-ways-to-Sunday sex."

CHAPTER SEVEN

HE DIDN'T CALL. After Brian had liquefied half her brain cells with that speech, and made it impossible for her to think of little else besides what more she could have done to get her sentence extended from six to *seven*-ways-to-Sunday sex...not one call or text all week.

She felt like an idiot.

Clearly, he was rethinking things between them. And the thought of that filled Tessa with a bone-deep feeling of loss, which was absurd really because he hadn't even been hers to lose.

Not hers to lose.

She repeated that mantra to herself as she picked up her ringing landline.

"Hello?"

"Tessa?"

She sighed. Still not hers to lose. "Hey Abby."

"Tessa, I promise I'm not playing cupid again. I really do need you to do me a favor if you can. Brian and I usually spend this day together every year. Doing nothing. It's a long story. And one that's not mine to tell. But I'm not feeling well and I don't want him to be alone today. Do you think you could go over in my place?"

"I really don't think—"

"Please, Tessa. I swear I don't have any ulterior motives here. I've never left Brian alone on this day for years. And you're the only one who I think will understand."

What if he doesn't want me to understand?

But she was wavering; Abby sounded so broken up about it. What could have possibly happened on such a specific day? She knew Beth hadn't died in the spring and unless Brian had some severe phobia of leprechauns, she didn't know what terrible thing could be plaguing him on March 17th.

"Why don't you ask Connor?"

"Because I think Brian would want to see you. In fact, I know he would. Now that I think about it, even if I weren't feeling under the weather, I'd still think you'd be the best person for this today."

So cryptic. "Okay, I'll be there."

⁂

BRIAN GLANCED at the clock and went over to answer the door, grabbing the phone along the way. He'd meant to call in the pizza order before Abby arrived, but somehow, he'd lost track of time. Seemed his mind was more distracted than usual today. But not with the usual distractions.

"Tessa."

He opened the door wider and Tessa swiftly ducked under his arm to let herself in uninvited with a determined, take-no-prisoners stride that was almost domineering enough to cover up the unsure set of her jaw.

Dammit, she was so freakin' *cute*.

"Tessa, what are you doing here?"

"Abby sent me."

For chrissakes, when had his best friend become such a meddler?

"She promised she's not playing matchmaker this time," interjected Tessa quickly. "She's not feeling well."

Now Brian was concerned. "Is she okay? Is my brother home with her?"

"Yes and yes. Abby said she's just been exhausted with her long work hours. Connor is apparently at home force-feeding her chicken soup and subjecting her to endless fussing. But she promised she'd call you tomorrow."

Tessa grabbed a throw pillow, plopped on the couch, and looked up at him expectantly, concern written all over her face. "So, do you want to tell me why Abby thinks I'm the best person to spend St. Patrick's Day with you? You don't have to tell me. But she seems to think I'd understand what you're going through."

He thought about that for a moment and shook his head. "I'm not sure you would. You didn't put your sister in a care home, did you? I remember Connor saying something about that once."

A sad look of understanding clouded over her face.

"No," she said quietly. "I didn't. I couldn't bear to leave her there alone."

That pierced him in the gut like a dull, serrated blade.

"Oh, Brian, I didn't mean—"

"No, it's okay. I did what I knew was best for Beth and Skylar. I couldn't be there to watch Beth all the time because I had to work. The care home took care of her in ways I couldn't." He gazed over at the calendar on the wall, at all the smiling green clovers Skylar had drawn on today's date. "March 17th was the day I admitted her. I remember it like it was yesterday. I remember signing all the paperwork, I remember not knowing how to leave, and most of all, I remember exactly what it felt like when I finally did. And sadly, at least for a while after that day, I know she remembered it all too."

"Her dementia hadn't set in yet?"

"It came in waves. But that day, she'd been fully lucid. I tell myself it's better than if the reverse had happened and she hadn't been aware when I left…that it would've been worse if she'd just woken up one day later with her mind crystal clear, but still wondering how in the hell she got there. No matter what I tell myself though, I can't ever forget *that look*—that look on Beth's face when I left the care home that night. Without her."

Remembering it hit him like a sucker punch every time. And he never blocked that blow, especially not on March 17th.

"I think Willow would've wanted to be put in a home."

Stunned, Brian looked over to see if she was just trying

to make him feel better.

Apparently not, because frankly, Tessa looked a little astonished herself. "I've never said that out loud before." She seemed to be chewing the words in her mouth before she asserted again, "But it's true. I think toward the end, before her memory started going, Willow actually did want to be put in a home. She tried to tell me once but I wouldn't hear of it." A self-deprecating sigh whooshed out of her. "It took me a few years to realize why she probably said it. My dad and I had arranged our work schedules so one of us would be at Willow's bedside at all times. I worked the bakery from 2 am to 11 am, and dad worked security at the lumberyard from 4 pm to midnight. It worked, but the schedule never really accounted for sleeping."

"Since dad had his own HD symptoms taking a little more out of him each day, I always made sure he got lots of rest. So, the only times I would sleep were the times he wasn't sleeping when he was home, which were only a few hours here and there. I remember I'd always be terrified to go to sleep. I was so sure something would happen to Willow if I did."

Her eyes slammed shut, the same way his did whenever he'd remember those types of memories. "And one day, I was proven right. I was sleeping when Willow had a massive seizure. I didn't even wake up. Luckily, my dad had just come home from work and he was able to call the ambulance in time."

"It was after that incident that Willow mentioned the care home." Gripping his hand in hers, she said softly, "I know it seems like our 'abandoning them' would be the worst thing they could feel. But when I looked at it from her perspective, from what she probably used to see every day in our exhausted faces, what she saw in my sobbing apologies when she woke up in the ICU..."

Tessa squeezed his hand gently. "So I guess I'm saying that at the end of the day, your way with the home, or my way without it, there was no winning or losing either way. Don't beat yourself up over it too much."

She chuckled lightly. "Says the pot to the kettle."

And just like that, the ice he'd built around his heart all day simply cracked right down the middle. He stared at her for a long moment and then asked, "Do you want to do something today?"

"BUT...ABBY SAID this was the day you two actively did nothing. Isn't it like a tradition for you two?"

"Until now, it has been. But really, it was her tradition that I adopted and applied to my own day of pain." His eyes ran over her face slowly. "I don't know...when I'm around you though, you're filled with such *life*. It's kind of inspiring. Plus, you make me laugh. You make me want to do *something* today. Is that okay?"

Smiling over that character profile, she wagered, "If I let you pick our activity, can I pick the meal?"

He chuckled. "Sure."

"Okay then, c'mon." She checked her watch. "There's

this great food truck over in Tempe that serves the best Southern food I've ever tasted. The guy puts the exact location where he's parked up on his twitter account every morning. It's kind of a thing. And I swear, no matter where he's parked, there's always a huge line." She hopped up off the couch. "If we book it over, we'll catch him before he's done for the day."

They were out the door seconds later, but were brought to a halt when her skirt got caught on the edge of the porch rail and tore at the back seam.

"I think Abby left a sewing kit in the house if you want to try and sew it up. Or you can stay here and I'll go get the food and come back."

"No, that's okay." She flipped her skirt around and studied the tear. Then she picked up the hem of her skirt, hooked her key in the tear, and let it rip.

Meanwhile, Brian was standing there just watching in fascination as she extended the tear all the way to the bottom of the skirt.

"You don't do anything normal, do you?"

"I make every effort not to." She flipped her skirt back around. "There, now it's a skirt with a long slit. It's cute. C'mon, let's go. Seriously, you have to taste this guy's shrimp and grits—"

He caught her by the elbow and spun her back into his arms. "You are so wonderfully weird," he murmured before leaning down to capture her mouth in a single unassuming, perfectly chaste kiss. That still managed to make her dizzy.

This time, it was Tessa who stopped them from heading out. "What's a few more minutes going to hurt?" she asked as she wrapped her arms around his neck and went in for multiple very assuming, perfectly unchaste kisses. To try and get *him* dizzy.

It was a great 'few minutes.'

But after it came and went, Brian being Brian groaned and pulled back. "Okay, no more of that for a while. I want you to get the meal choice you want. And if we continue more of *that*, we'll both starve to death."

He gave her a lopsided grin—likely at the loopy expression she was undoubtedly wearing—and tugged her toward the car. She barely remembered buckling the seatbelt.

"So, serious question," he tossed out when they were out on the road, "after we eat, can I pick what we were just doing as one of our activities for the night?" His brows rose suggestively.

"I don't see why not," she shrugged and replied without thinking, "Because if you hadn't so rudely interrupted us back there, I was all set to just throw on some fruit-flavored chapstick and call it a meal."

He laughed, shaking his head. "I'm really glad you came over today, sweetie."

⁂

HOURS LATER, Tessa was walking hand in hand with Brian back to the car, merrily giving him consolation bites of her giant ice cream cone—her prize for beating him at bowling after their just-made-it-in-time food truck dinner, which he'd loved as much as she'd hoped he would. The goofy smile on her face had less to do with the ice cream, and more to do with his perfectly *outrageous* accusation that she'd cheated all throughout the bowling game.

No one had ever accused her of using, letting alone *having* 'feminine wiles' before.

She liked it.

When they finally got to the car, Brian, ever the gentleman, opened Tessa's passenger door and helped her in. It wasn't until after she was buckled in and floating on a post-perfect date bubble, however, that he leaned in and said, "Okay, so tell me about your rules for flings."

Startled, she blinked at him and felt her pulse triple at the transformation.

His usual guy next door eye twinkle? Gone. Now, it was wholly eclipsed by the slow burning dare-you-to-guess-what-I'm-thinking smolder she'd been fantasizing about since she'd seen it last. Eight days ago, if she wasn't mistaken.

"The other week, you said you weren't looking for anything serious," he continued as she sat there, searching for her long lost ability to speak. "Connor used to have a one-month parameter on his flings; I figured you must have some specifics as well. And I'm curious to know what they are."

Crap. She was simply not this good at improvising on the fly. Especially not when she had absolutely no frame of reference, and exactly one sexual experience in her past.

She should just tell him the truth.

"Okay," he admitted, "I'm not just curious, I'm interested. Like you said, we have a connection, and since I've recently been thinking of trying my brother's dating methods—seemed to work great for him—I thought I'd put it out there and ask you flat-out if you're interested."

Was she interested? Um. That was a no-brainer. "Yes."

He grinned. "Great. Do you want to get together next Friday? The girls will be at Becky's for a sleepover until Sunday. I can meet you at your place and you can tell me all your fling parameters then."

Next weekend. Fabulous.

That gave her one whole week to study up on flings.

☙❦❧

TAKING A SEAT on the couch in Tessa's apartment, Brian eyed a stack of chick flick DVDs on the side table that he was actually surprised to see in Tessa's collection, along with a notebook filled with notes, and a neatly written, short, but…interesting list.

RULES FOR FLING
1) No sleeping over (the guest flingee must depart before the resident flinger wakes up)
2) No making plans further than one week in advance
3) No two consecutive date nights in a row
4) No telling Skylar or Connor or Abby
5) No sex in each other's beds (the ground, sofa, countertops, hotel beds are fine)

Criminy, she just kept getting cuter every day.

"So is there someplace for me to sign on this contract?" he called out.

"What?" She returned from the kitchen with two beers and gasped in horror. "Ohmigod, put that down. That was...just a draft."

"Uh huh." Oh boy, this was just too much fun. "What's the deal with number one? That's a little harsh. What happens if the guy doesn't wake up as early as you? I know I myself like to sleep in late."

"Well...then I'd kick you so you'd wake up, and then I'd go back to sleep." A victorious little 'so-*there*' glimmer lit her eyes.

So adorable.

"Geez, I bet that was fun for all your past flings," he editorialized casually, grinning when she balked. That was the exact reaction he'd been looking for. "But one night stands sleep over all the time, don't they?"

"And that's my point," she recovered quickly. "One night stands are awkward the next day. Plus, they're singular events—you never expect to see them again. Which is why a fling has to be handled differently."

Not bad. Considering she'd just pulled that one out of her ass on the fly. Clearly, he'd underestimated her.

Remembering Connor's addendum on his one-monthers, he then threw more chips in the pile and raised with, "So what's your policy on notes? You know, for the guest flingee who sneaks out before the resident flinger wakes up? Connor used to have a strict no notes, calls, texts, emails, or tokens of affection rule."

"*What?*" Her riled scowl was on behalf of all womankind. "How that man never got drilled in the nuts by a stiletto is beyond me. Of course leave a note. I mean, it doesn't have to be a sonnet or anything. Just short and casual...rhyming optional."

Brian hid his grin. For the umpteenth time since they'd met, he thought about just how fantastically different Tessa was from Beth and Abby.

When he'd first met Beth back in high school, he'd been a nervous wreck—his heart had started racing the second she'd said hello, and absolute gibberish had spewed out of his mouth in response. Abby, on the other hand, had been an easy fit from the start; from that first day of college, he'd felt like he'd known her forever and had been completely relaxed around her.

Meeting Tessa, however, had been like getting whacked upside the head with a club. He'd felt blindsided by her, *unsettled* around her almost at first sight, definitely at first speak. She made him feel off-balance. And borderline ornery. She got under his skin with frightening ease, and managed to find bizarre, hidden access points to his heart just as effortlessly. Around Tessa, he more often than not found himself doing things he normally wouldn't do.

Like agreeing to have a fling with a 'fling expert' who'd clearly never been flung before.

Reaching over for a pen on the coffee table, he initialed

next to the title of her list. "Okay, I'm in."

While Tessa was busy gaping at his initials, Brian took the opportunity to unravel more of the enigma that was Tessa Daniels. Basically, he started snooping. He dropped a kiss on her parted lips and headed over to the bookshelf near the kitchen to look at the small handful of memorabilia and even smaller handful of photos. There was one photo with her sister and her dad, one of just her dad when he was older, one of Willow sitting at a piano, and another with Tessa and her sister in a hospital bed, each with matching pink streaks in their hair.

Another mystery solved.

He gently picked up the old three-ring binder propped next to the piano picture of Willow. "Are these her compositions?" There were a few dozen at least, all in plastic protectors.

As if his words had finally shaken her out of her stupor, Tessa came to join him by the bookshelf. "Yes. In chronological order, each one like a special musical page of her life, from what I could remember. I used to love listening to her play."

"Did you ever play?"

"No. I, um, didn't get a chance to do any extracurriculars."

Right, because their lives had always revolved around Willow.

Christ, her childhood had been a sad one.

When he heard his fierce little survivor clearing her

throat to get his attention, he turned to see her gripping her list of rules in her hands, her face utterly serious, "Brian, about these—"

Just then, that familiar musical ringtone—*seriously*, where did he know that song from—rang out from her bag.

"Dammit. Hang on." She rushed off to go answer her phone.

Hearing her enter her bedroom to take the call, Brian took a long, sweeping look around Tessa's apartment once again. Everything about it was stark, bare. Not at all the type of vibrant home he'd expect from her. Likewise for her bookshelf. He couldn't help but compare it to the bookshelf of memories at his own house that was bursting at the seams, and groaning over the weight of all the photo frames they kept cramming onto it.

"It's not as filled as yours," she commented softly from behind him, as if reading his mind. "I haven't added anything to it in years. There haven't really been any new memories to collect. Or anyone to share them with." She took a deep breath, and once again, that determined, hope-filled, me-against-the-world smile was back on her face.

The woman was just too good at dealing with life's unjust realities on her own.

He wished she'd let him help her.

"Brian, I hate to cut our night short but that was work on the phone just now. Looks like I'm going to have to pull an all-nighter. One of our freelancers bailed at the last minute and they don't have any articles in the bank to cover this specific topic for the summer edition." With a frustrated huff, she scooped up her hair and tied it up into a tight bun. "Since the cover is already locked, that means I need to write the article. Easier said than done, of course, since I have absolutely no experience with the topic. But I'll figure something out."

"What's the topic?" he asked, wanting to help somehow.

A slow, brightening sparkle entered her eyes as she turned to gaze at him in a whole new light. "Camping."

He beamed. "Well then today's your lucky day. Because standing right before you is a bonafide camping connoisseur who has absolutely no marketable writing skills to speak of, and will very likely get completely distracted by the gorgeous editor in charge."

She chuckled. "You're hired."

─────

NINE LONG, CRAZY-STRESSFUL hours later, Tessa was emailing the article in for submission, and Brian was half-dozing on the double-wide recliner. Damn, the thing was comfortable—he'd have to look into getting one for his house, he thought to himself muzzily.

Better yet, he could just move hers into his place, owner and all.

Huh.

There were those crazy, random thoughts again.

Tonight, he was blaming it on exhaustion.

"Okay, the issue's locked." When Tessa returned and

shuffled by to plop down on the sofa opposite the recliner, he scooped her up by the waist, pulled her across his lap and tucked her right next to him.

Perfect fit.

She cuddled against his chest. "Thank you so much, Brian. There's no way I would've been able to do that article without you."

"My pleasure. But you really didn't have to give me a byline."

"Of course I did. You came up with most of it." She cat-yawned. "Are you hungry? Do you want me to make you a sandwich or something?"

"If I say yes will you actually be able to get up and do it?" he teased, eyes slipping closed with a groan as he pressed the side button to slide the recliner back fully.

"Good point," she murmured, snuggling into him sleepily.

Yawning, he held her close and started drifting off.

"Brian?"

"Hmmm?"

"Are you going to keep poking me with that thing all night?"

"As long as you're lying on top of me? Yes."

She burrowed deeper and twined her legs with his. "Okay."

And that was the last thing he remembered before sleep overtook him.

CHAPTER EIGHT

SHE WAS SO WARM.

With a murmur of pleasure, Tessa slowly rubbed her face against the source of the heat, feeling her skin come alive on contact.

"A man can only take so much torture, Tessa." The low, rough voice pierced through the sleepy fog she was still floating in, but not enough to make the delicious feelings go away. She shifted her hips and felt something hard brush against her inner thigh.

"Brian," she sighed.

The arms that had been cradling her as if she were a newborn kitten, suddenly turned to steel.

"Tessa, wake up," he commanded, straight out of her most wicked fantasies.

Her alpha man was back. When was the last time she'd dreamt of him? Oh right, last night...and every night before that for weeks.

For some reason, tonight felt different though. More real. Infinitely sexier.

She smiled against his hot skin and felt a groan rumbling up the column of his throat. Nuzzling against his jaw, she felt reckless enough tonight to test her dream's boundaries, to push past her own. Sliding her body fully atop his, she reveled at the feel of all those hot, hardened muscles.

Especially that one.

"Godammit, woman." Strong, thick fingers speared through her hair and cradled her skull as the hottest lips she'd ever felt started searing every nerve ending she didn't even know she had all along her neck. "If you don't wake up and stop smiling like the cat who caught the canary, I won't be held accountable for my actions."

Jolting awake finally, Tessa forced her eyes open.

And found herself drowning in the most intense sea blue eyes she'd ever seen.

"*Brian.*"

He bucked against her hips. "Stop saying my name like that," he rumbled, his pupils dilating right before her eyes, his chest rising and falling raggedly beneath her hands.

Pushing herself up fully, she froze when she felt the hard ridge of his erection nudging urgently between her thighs.

"Don't. Move." His eyelids slammed shut, and harsh lines of tension etched across his face as he held her immobile above him.

"Brian—" She scooted forward for better leverage.

Before she could so much as yelp, he sat up fully and yanked her torso against him, his brawny arms encasing her in a cocoon of heat, as every inch of his hard sculpted chest and eight-pack abs sealed her tight against his body.

"You suck at following directions," he growled.

Guilty as charged. Then again, where in the world has he been that he was only now getting that memo?

As she attempted to follow directions then, she also began taking inventory of the changes in Brian. Seeing the hard edge of desire in his eyes was...intoxicating.

She wanted more.

Later, she'd wonder over her sanity for pushing the man when he looked this *primal*. But for now...

She reached up and shaped her hands over tan, chiseled features, smiling when his hips jerked up against hers in reflex as she slid her tongue along the taut line of his lips. A sharp jaw clench beneath her fingers and then *nothing*.

His harsh breathing had to mean he was as affected as she was, and yet the man still continued to sit there. Brooding. All but vibrating with hot alpha sex waves while he continued to look at her like he wanted to devour her...but just plain wasn't going to.

Unable, unwilling to wait any longer for him to make the first move, she took control and shifted her hips forward, wanting that snug, rigid fit.

Forward and back, forward and back.

She became lightheaded as the searing sensations started rushing throughout her system, causing her to pulse against him just as he pulsed right back against her.

After a while, it became less about inciting his hunger, and more about feeding her own. An altogether unfamiliar craving, seeing as how she hadn't had sex besides that one time in high school, and she never really got into 'taking care of business' on her own.

Clearly, she'd been missing out.

Her hands fisted in his shirt and her eyes drifted shut. Now if she just angled her hips...

Holy hell.

A vicious, guttural sound from deep in Brian's chest broke her concentration. But then the feeling of flying that came when he shot up to his feet and pushed her back against the couch, seconds before he started yanking his clothes off soon had her concentration focused on newer, better things. Wow.

Tense, sculpted muscles as far as the eye could see, rippling and clenching.

"Clothes off," he rasped, reaching down to drag her shirt up off her body.

Front-clasp bras were now her new favorite thing— Brian's too, judging by the volatile explosion of lust in his eyes that detonated the instant she was fully bared to his gaze.

"So beautiful."

She felt the rough, graveled words repeated against her neck, moments before his mouth closed over her nipple and sent pleasure lashing across her senses. With lips, tongue, and teeth, he tasted, explored, incited. Soon, her nails were scoring down his back and his teeth were nipping at her in symphony.

"I need to be inside of you *now*."

Tessa didn't even realize he'd slid off her jeans and panties until she felt him slip back between her legs. The tiny gasp she'd been unable to keep buried at the skin-on-skin contact had him gripping her hips and rocking his full length against her core.

"Jesus, I could come just from the feel of you spilling over me," he rumbled against her skin. "You're so damn responsive."

His mouth came over hers again almost desperately, stealing what little oxygen she had left directly from its source as his thumb moved from the blade of her hipbone across her soft mound. Lower, and lower.

Her whole body corded like a bow. "*Brian!*"

CHRIST, HE'D ALMOST come right then and there.

The way Tessa said his name went to his head faster than whiskey. And the snug grip and slick, wet glide of her sex over his violently sensitive head was his drunken undoing. He forced himself back and grabbed for the condom in his jeans. Sliding the rubber in place, he was back in a flash. Thank God he'd allowed himself that line of wishful thinking when he'd left his house this evening.

She was watching him all the while beneath long dark lashes, her full, soft lips parted in anticipation.

"Not sure I can be gentle this first time, sweetheart."

"I don't want gentle," came her heated reply. "I've been fantasizing about you since I first heard your voice on the phone, growling. Your voice has been the one in my head, my dreams. Hearing you lose control…"

It was no use, he had to have her. Latching his mouth onto one pebbled nipple, he plunged into her in one deep thrust.

And froze when she cried out in what sounded like pain.

"*Dammit.* Did I hurt you?" He ground his teeth and started sliding back out of her. Jesus. So control-thievingly tight. "God, I'm so sorry, sweetheart. Are you alright?"

"No, don't stop," she managed on a gasp, wrapping her legs around his waist to keep him from pulling out completely.

He shuddered as he sank back in partway. "Honey, you're so tight. I didn't know. I wasn't thinking."

"Not your fault." Her voice sounded strained. "I've only

had sex that one time. Born again virgin," she joked, breath hissing in at the effort.

He dropped his forehead down to hers. "Good lord, why didn't you tell me? I would've gone slower. Gotten you wetter."

She shifted under him with an expression he could only describe as utter skepticism.

"Um." More doubt marred that now very serious pixie face of hers. "Honestly, Brian, I don't think you could've gotten me all that much wetter," she informed him finally, sounding like she was breaking the tragic news that the Easter Bunny wasn't real.

Despite the fact that half his shaft was buried inside of her in the most agonizing pleasure he'd ever experienced, he chuckled over that. Clearly, his little 'expert flinger' was even far less of an expert than he'd thought. "Sweetheart, I'm definitely going to take you up on that dare you just issued. But not now." Silently praying for strength, he drew back out a bit. "Because right now, I'm about two seconds from exploding." He slid his hand between them to circle his thumb over her sensitive nub and exhaled in relief when he heard her breath break, the tension in her legs relax a little.

"We'll start again. But we'll go slow." *Painfully slow.*

Even if it killed him.

He slid into her again, gently this time, starting an achingly unhurried rhythm even though he was nearly shaking with the intense need to take her hot and fast, possess her completely.

Soon, however, he deemed the loss of his sanity a worthwhile sacrifice when he felt the sweetness of her response rain over him. Soft, feathery whimpers against his neck with each liquid stroke, the sweetest broken cries he could imagine, and then pure, naked bliss as she arched to meet him thrust for thrust.

When he finally felt her orgasm start to rip through her, he lost it completely.

Bracing one hand against the back of the couch, the other on her hip, he sheathed his entire length in her in one long, hard plunge. Deep. Again and again. Without an ounce of control. Until she clamped down on him and started riding him just as desperately, her tiny inner pulses driving him past sanity, beyond civility.

He ground his teeth to keep from shouting. Heart hammering, red-hot pleasure racing down his spine, he drove into her one last time and reveled in the feel of her snug channel pulsing like crazy all around him as he went roaring over the edge.

Before everything went black.

⚜

BRIAN OPENED HIS EYES and for a second, forgot where he was. When he heard a shower faucet shut off and saw Tessa's sweet frame in the bathroom at the end of the hall, only just barely visible by the small nightlight next to the sink, it all came back to him in a rush.

He got up and headed over to her, stopping to lean against the doorframe with a smile when she continued the towel drying extravaganza, completely oblivious to his presence.

"Were you just showering in the dark?"

She jerked her head up and jammed the two ends of the towel back around her.

Shame.

"Yes," she replied breathlessly.

As he waited patiently for the rest of her answer, she shrugged, drawing his attention to her naked shoulders. All that soft, damp skin was making it hard to remember what he'd originally asked her.

"I rarely shower with the light on. It's a habit I never thought to stop."

Right. Okay, back to her reasons for showering in the dark.

She shrugged again. "Willow was usually napping when I'd get home from the bakery. The only other bathroom besides the one connected to her room was downstairs and since I didn't like leaving her unattended even for the fifteen minutes it'd take to stop smelling like cake and feeling like a loaf of bread, I always just showered in the dark to avoid waking her up."

"It's not that weird," she defended before he could even get a thought in edgewise. She shoved her hands on her hips, unknowingly shifting the towel up those amazing legs of hers, and effectively causing him to lose track of the conversation again. "It's not like I need the light on to be able to run a washcloth over my own body."

Well hell, the image *that* provoked just derailed his focus completely.

And got him hard so fast he was reeling from a headrush as he stepped forward to trace a finger over the top edge of her towel. "I like that you shower in the dark. In fact, I was thinking of joining the movement. Save on electricity, help the planet and all." Dipping in the valley between her breasts to loosen her towel, he suggested huskily, "How about you and I save on electricity together, right now?"

Lashes fluttering down as she watched his hands at work, she murmured distractedly, "B-but I already finished."

Grinning, he slid his hand past the opening of the towel and up her inner thigh. "Did you, Tessa? Did you finish in there? Without me?" he teased, intentionally misunderstanding her. "Guess I'm going to have to work a whole lot harder at proving to you that I can in fact get you *much* wetter." The catch in her breathing just propelled him forward as he edged her back into the shower stall. "Luckily, I do like a good challenge." He tugged the towel open fully and skimmed it off her body, tossing it on the bathroom rug before sliding the shower door shut.

The glass door was only slightly frosted but still, closing it encased them in near pitch darkness.

He felt her jump when he whispered in her ear, "I forgot the washcloth. So you'll just have to settle for me running my hands over your body instead." Though he couldn't see her expression, he felt her thighs clench tight in reply as his hands wandered over her hips.

With a flick of his wrist, he reached behind her and turned the hot water on, adjusting the spray to send sheets of steaming hot water cascading down her back, streaming over her shoulders to drench her front as he slid his slick palms over all her dainty little curves.

When the steam quickly dropped their visibility down to zero, all his other senses took over and *demanded* he stop letting the water have all the fun. He turned the faucet off and fell to his knees, his lips following a detour-filled path down her torso before pausing to sip at the gentle hollow of her navel. "You have no idea how sexy you are." Shaking his head in wonder, he trailed his way down to her soft mound.

And caught her when her knees buckled.

His tongue dipped lower, just once, before he looked up and whispered against her heated core, "Now, let's see about that challenge you threw down earlier…"

TESSA WAS ALL BUT SITTING on his biceps, her back against shower wall, and her fingers threaded in his hair as he slowly, tortuously proved to her over and over again that her earlier assertion had been *very* wrong. She was most definitely wetter now. So much so that she wasn't even blushing over the logistics of her seating arrangement. For now.

Of course, with the kinds of thoughts currently bombarding her brain, blushing would be completely contradictory.

She didn't know how much more she could take.

He'd been torturing her for who knows how long now, bringing her right up to the brink three times, before easing off, simply to build her right back up again.

The bastard.

When his tongue began its decadent torment for a fourth time, it was quite possible she *demanded* that he let her come. The details were a bit fuzzy. All she knew was that she was set to take matters into her own hands for the first time ever when *finally,* she felt two thick fingers slide into her as his mouth closed tight and—

Fireworks exploded throughout her body.

She only just barely remembered to stifle her scream so she didn't wake the neighbors. In the whole neighborhood.

At least twenty different kinds of instruments in a full symphony orchestra resounded in her ears. Ocean waves crested. And angels with brand new wings sang pitch-perfect high notes alongside floating harps and oddly enough, Caribbean steel drums.

It took several long minutes for her to coast back down to reality.

His soft kisses on her inner thighs were helping the process along, but it was also making it so she was becoming ready for him to prove her wrong all over again.

"Okay fine," she admitted in a husky, wholly satisfied voice she hardly recognized. "You win. You were right."

His pleased chuckles against her still-feverish flesh were

serving to get her all worked up once more with unreasonable ease so she quickly moved to slide her thighs off his shoulders.

Aaand there was the delayed blushing.

She covered her cheeks with her hands even though there was no way he could possibly see that in the dark.

"You're blushing right now aren't you?" He was smiling, she could hear it. "You're so damn cute."

And for some reason, that made her go a little nutty.

She wanted to be more than *cute* for him.

With a deep, steadying breath, she dropped her right hand down to the hard, hot rise of his erection. And boy was it hard.

Looks like she wasn't the only one getting tortured the entire time.

Having never done this before, she decided to jump in feet-first, relying on the few romance novels she'd read in her life to guide her as she slowly slid her hand up and down his shaft. Squeezing every once in a while out of sheer curiosity.

Soon, the sound of his low, deep groans bouncing off the tiles served to be so much more rewarding than a gold star for her efforts.

"So now are you going to challenge me to make *you* wetter?" she asked, getting seriously drunk off seeing Brian practically *panting*.

"Tessa, you don't want to play this game right now."

She swiped her thumb over the tip of him. "But I think I do," she tossed back, licking her thumb and shivering at the taste of him. "You got a chance to taste me." Falling to her knees, she kissed the granite cut grooves carved into the slant of his hips, and pressed her lips across the sexy tan line at the base of his abs before finally building up the nerve to run her tongue along his entire length in one languid stroke.

"Now it's my turn to taste you."

⁂

BRIAN WAS SO GOING TO make her pay.

Definitely. The very second he was no longer at her complete and total mercy. Whenever the hell that was going to be. A long while from now, he estimated—hopefully—as he watched the curious little vixen get him back and then some, having a grand old time with what he was pretty sure was her first blow job.

She was a natural.

She'd just gotten through blowing a damp, teasing breath over him while speaking in some mysterious language his bloodless brain had failed to recognize, and now her hot little fist was effectively pumping him past the breaking point.

The tortuous little siren damn well knew it too.

Because this time, when he felt the slick silk of her mouth surround his beyond-hard flesh, she didn't just torment him with shy, liquid velvet promises.

This time, she took him as deep as she could go.

"You're playing with fire, honey," he managed to grate out, jaw clenched, breathing shot, voice savagely coarse. He wasn't going to last much longer. Especially not when, instead of heeding his warning, the evil woman placed both hands on his hips and took him even *deeper*.

"Tessa," he growled, "I'm going to come in your mouth if you don't stop."

And what did his gorgeous first-timer do with *that* public service announcement?

She stopped breathing for a brief second, and then released a quiet moan with him deep in her throat.

For chrissakes.

With a limited supply of oxygen sawing in and out of his chest, every muscle in his body went rigid as a surge of heat rushed down his spine and whipped across his nerve endings.

It took absolutely everything in him not to let go, not to take her mouth harder and faster, not to give in to the wild, primitive lust filling his veins. He only just barely fought his way back from the edge.

But then he saw the sheer, naked pleasure shining in her eyes.

And everything spontaneously combusted.

His release detonated through him in shards of scorching hot shrapnel. A loud roar filled his head as firebursts of lights exploded behind his eyelids.

Never had he come so hard in his life.

Hand braced against the wall to keep himself upright, he willed his heart rate to slow back down to a near-human pounding. It took a while. But when his ears finally did stop buzzing, his still-recovering brain eventually registered that *he* was the source of the low, feral sounds of raw, male satisfaction echoing around the bathroom.

And that the one content, soft little sigh he just heard had come from Tessa.

⋘⋙

SNUGGLED UP ON THE COUCH, making sleepy chitchat, Tessa wondered what normal flingers do when the night was winding down.

It didn't seem like Brian had any intention of going anywhere. Weirdly enough. But since they were out of condoms, she honestly didn't see what more fling-sanctioned activities they could do for the rest of the night.

And on the tail end of that thought, it occurred to her that she didn't have the first clue what his normal protocol was in this type of situation because they'd never discussed *his* rules for flings. A horrible oversight, which, in hindsight, could've saved her a lot of research if she'd just let him present his rules first.

Before she could gear up to broach the topic to him, however, Brian's attention was snagged by her little memorabilia collection next to the TV. He sat forward, peering at the lunch pails and thermoses and random trinkets on the top shelf in surprise. "Never would've pictured you for an old school Saturday morning cartoon collector."

Grinning, she shook her head. "I'm not. Those were actually Willow's old lunch pails and toys that got handed down to me." She smiled up at the *Muppet Babies* thermos and old school *Strawberry Shortcake* pencil case. "But just because I'm not a collector doesn't mean I'm not a card carrying fan of '80s cartoons. Because I am. *If* you haven't noticed by my t-shirts."

"*SilverHawks!*" he exclaimed then, out of the clear blue sky.

She chuckled, inordinately pleased with his outburst.

"That's your ringtone on your phone, isn't it? I knew I recognized that music. Man, I used to love that show when I was a kid."

"It's on Cartoon Network. When I used to stay up late to keep an eye on Willow while she was asleep, I'd have myself a little '80s cartoon fest. It was actually a lot of fun."

He grabbed the remote and pulled her against him on the couch. "Well it's three a.m. now. Let's see if there are some good cartoons on before we go to bed."

Something warm and fuzzy expanded in her chest then, even as her brain registered that the *we* in the going-to-bed part was probably a flagrant fling violation for her stupid 'rules.'

She sighed and was just about to mention it when he tilted his head at her and asked, "Hey, I meant to ask, since we fell asleep working earlier, did we already break your first fling rule? You're not pissed are you?"

Good question. One she should probably know the answer to. "Um…"

"I mean I know our sleeping right now wouldn't be a big deal since it's pretty much morning but last night's little nap session was definitely during the p.m. hours. I thought I'd better get a clarification."

And a clarification you shall get. As soon as she figured it out.

Geez, she hated these rules.

Before she could even begin to make up something that would sound like a logical answer, however, the question king fired off another one, "Oh, and since our date last night was interrupted, if I want to just stay here so I can hang out with you again tonight, that wouldn't be breaking your consecutive-night rule would it?"

Another humdinger. "Well..."

"Because if we already broke those two rules, I don't see the harm in breaking the no-bed rule," he finished with a broad smile she felt nuzzling against her cheek.

It was possible the man was on to her.

"Okay, okay," she fessed up, "so those aren't exactly *my* rules."

"You don't say." His smile moved up to her temple and turned into a gentle kiss.

"And perhaps 'expert' was a bit of a stretch in terms of my fling repertoire."

"Yeah," he chuckled, sounding pleased, "I kind of got that."

She pulled back and gazed into his eyes curiously. "What gave me away?" She'd thought she did pretty a good job during his vetting process.

"My first clue was all those dvd rentals and notebook.

Either you were fibbing just a tiny bit about the flinging, or you were in some sort of player cult and you had a book report due on Monday."

She felt her cheeks flush bright red. "Then why'd you sign that list and play along?"

"Because I like you. A lot. And I want to be with you. So if I need to sign my initials next to a bunch of rules I had every intention of breaking anyway, I didn't see what the big deal was."

Her lips twitched to the side. The guy was just too much.

With no retort for him in sight, she did what she always did when her brain went on the blink—she simply said the first thing that popped into her head. "There's a good chance I'm going to get attached to you if you're not careful."

He kissed the tip of her nose. "Well then you'll have good company."

CHAPTER NINE

TESSA TOOK A DEEP BREATH and hit send on the number she'd been staring at for the last five minutes, wondering over her sanity for even going through with this.

"Hello?"

"Hey mom."

"Tessa?"

She flinched. It was always a small kick in the shins when she heard that puzzled question mark.

"Yes, mom. It's me, Tessa." *The only one I know of who calls you mom.* She shoved down that unwelcome-stray-dog feeling and asked brightly, "How've you been? How's the new job?"

"Oh, it's going spectacularly. My sales numbers are through the roof."

Sales numbers? Ah, so this was a new, new job. "I take it the advertising focus group job was a bust?"

"Oh *that* job? That was ages ago. My goodness, when did I talk to you last?"

"Um...I left you a message around Christmas, then

again to wish you a Happy New Year."

But you never called back.

"Well that explains it. Over the past few months, your mother has quickly become one of South Beach Miami's rising stars in the feminine beauty product sales catalog biz. They're even going to let me start crossing over to some of the male beauty product lines as well. Isn't that fabulous?"

The feat of her mother sticking out a job for a few months was in fact, pretty fabulous. "That's great, mom. And you really sound happy about this one."

"Oh, I am. This is definitely my calling."

One of her many. Her 'calling' last summer had been radio commercial acting. And before that, it had been a phone service rep position that she'd deemed perfect because all it had required her to do was read out of a manual. But of course, she'd quit the job three days later because, well, all it had required her to do was read out of a manual.

The worst of the bunch had been the work-from-home scam from three years ago. That one had ended with Tessa having to wire five thousand dollars to her mother to tide her over until the sports equipment testing job finally panned out.

This stroll down memory lane was seriously bumming her out. "So mom, I met this guy," she blurted out then, cutting to the chase.

"Oh honey, how wonderful! You haven't dated in… Wow, when *was* the last time you dated?"

That would be never. Thanks for remembering. She sighed. "Anyway, like I was saying, I met someone—"

"Give me all the details," came the quick and surprisingly attentive reply. "What's he do for a living?"

"He's a high school business teacher."

"Good, good, so he's not a freeloader. Those are fun to play with for a night, but getting rid of them can be such a pain."

As utterly bizarre as this conversation was, this was actually the longest and most engaged conversation Tessa could ever recall them having. Dropping onto her couch, she settled in and tried to wrap her brain around the entire experience.

"Is he handsome? Does he work out a lot? Ooh, what color are his eyes? I'm always a sucker for sexy eyes."

Tessa's mind did a few more flips before she got her bearings and replied, "Yes, he's absolutely gorgeous. Errr…I'm assuming he works out a lot because he's also a football coach at the high school where he works." Was that a squeal on the other end of the phone line? So surreal. "And his eyes are amazing—an ocean blue most of the time."

"Oh, he sounds just yummy. I'm so happy for you, dear."

Irrationally, Tessa felt like she was going to start crying. She couldn't remember the last time her mother had ever been so attentive, so affectionate.

"His name is Brian, by the way. And he has a fantastic daughter in middle school."

A stark pause and then an almost horrified, "*A daughter?* Oh, Tessa, no."

Aaand, they were back. The way her mother said her name- never failed to make her feel two inches tall and far more than a dollar short.

"*Tessa*, you can't date a man with a child. You won't be able to avoid getting serious."

She paused a beat before admitting, "What if I'm thinking of getting serious?"

Her mother gasped. "You can*not* be thinking of having a long term relationship with this man, Tessa. It's just not right. You know as well as I do that this would just end in heartbreak for everyone involved. Especially if he has a daughter. He's probably looking for…well, someone a little different from you."

"He and Skylar both know about my being a dropout, mom. He didn't think anything of it."

"So you've told him *everything*?"

Tessa remained silent.

"That's what I thought. Have a heart. Don't take this any further. He sounds like a very nice man who deserves better."

Better than me.

"Tessa, you know I love you. And you know I want you to be happy. But not at the expense of someone else. Besides, why are you even looking for something serious anyway? Look at my life. A hot, brand new model every few months to drive around, nothing to tie me down. The world is my oyster. I couldn't be happier. Take it from me, there is simply no better way to live."

Tessa could think of a thousand better ways to live.

And she could picture Brian in every single scenario.

"I know you think I'm wrong about this, but I also know that you *know* I'm right. You should just end it now. Before it's too late. Let the man be happy."

Right, because he'd be miserable with me. She couldn't take anymore. "Mom, I've got to get going. I forgot I need to head over to the care home in a half hour."

"Oh, that's nice. You're still doing that volunteer work?"

Everything HD related was always 'volunteer work' to her mother; she simply couldn't comprehend it in any other context. So it didn't really matter whether she answered her or not. "I really got to go. Thanks for chatting with me, mom."

"Alright, well good luck with everything. Remember, it's always better to just rip the band-aid off. And darling, you know you don't have to thank me. That's what I'm here for."

Tessa wasn't going to touch that one.

"Bye, mom."

෴

BRIAN CAME BACK in from his morning run and knew something was wrong the second he stepped foot in the door.

He was already racing across the house to Skylar's bedroom, the muffled sounds of her crying slashing him with blades of paralyzing fear. He practically took the door off its hinges as he burst through, expecting to see a scene not unlike a post-apocalyptic disaster zone.

"Sky-bug, what's the matter?" He eased over to her window seat, where she was curled in a tight ball, trying her best to get her crying under control. "Are you hurt?"

"I c-can't s-stop," she stuttered, her breathing heaving in and out uncontrollably.

Brian ran out to the kitchen and returned with a paper bag. Holding it over her mouth, he squeezed her hand and said in the calmest voice he could, "Just breathe, honey. Keep your eyes on me and just breathe nice and easy, in and out. Don't think about anything else except for the sound of your breathing." He nodded encouragingly when her gasping breaths started to slow. Removing the bag, he continued in a soothing murmur, "Okay now we have to do the belly breathing; remember how we used to help mom? Slow deep breath in through your nose, fill your belly up with air…and then out through your mouth. Good, just like that. Just a few more, take your time."

Meanwhile, Brian was on the verge of hyperventilating himself.

The five minutes it took for Skylar's breathing to return to normal felt like the longest of his life.

"How you doing?" he asked gently when her eyes were no longer the size of saucers. "Ready for a glass of water?"

Skylar nodded, exhausted, and slumped against the wall while he went to get her a drink.

It took far more restraint than he thought he possessed to remain silent as he watched her ease back out of her panic attack. Remembering how walking used to help Beth, and wanting to give Skylar a change in environment just in case that was the trigger, he held out his hand. "C'mon, let's get some fresh air in the backyard."

By the time they were both seated in the gazebo, she was looking relatively calm.

"You want to tell me what happened back there?"

Her gaze dropped to the ground, and she shrugged half-heartedly. "It's nothing."

"That was *not* nothing, sweetie. Do you need me to call your therapist? Schedule you an emergency appointment?"

At her smothered cringe, he grew even more confused. "Are you having a problem with Dr. Gibson?" Skylar had been going once a week for over a year now and never had he heard any complaints from either side.

"No, I just... I'm having a hard time talking to her lately." She slid her focus over to the orchid plants woven into the far end of the gazebo. "I feel like we talk about the same things every week and…it's like she can't hear me, like no one can hear me. Except for Becky. And Tessa."

Brian tensed. "So this is about the gene testing again?"

"Not just the gene testing. It's all of it." She shook her head and looked away. "You just don't get it. None of you get it." Her voice was starting to sound panicked again.

"They *can't* get it, sweetie," called out a calm voice approaching them. "Not unless you explain it to them."

They both looked up to see Tessa walking across the lawn to join them.

When did she get here?

"Skylar texted me while you were on your run," she explained, at his questioning look. "I got here as quickly as I could and I let myself in. You left the front door ajar."

He had?

Everything had been such a blur. Still was. Skylar had been talking for nearly ten minutes now and he still didn't have a clue how to help her.

Tessa sat down on the railing opposite of them and said quietly, "Skylar, it's not that they don't want to hear you, it's that they can't understand what you're going through. You need to explain it to your doctors, to your father. I know you think they should get it because they already saw your mom go through it, but I guarantee you, they don't." Her eyes landed on his as she continued, "So just start from what you feel like when you wake up every day. Describe it if you can't explain it. And go from there."

Brian watched in horror as tears filled Skylar's eyes again. How had he not known his little girl was going through so much agony? "I'm listening, honey. And I promise I'll hear you. Just...talk to me, please."

"It's not every morning," Skylar whispered as she looked up at Tessa, almost as if reaching for a lifeline before repeating, "It's not every morning, but some mornings I wake up and I wonder if today's going to be the day that I'll know for sure if I have HD or not. And for the five or ten minutes that I sit there and think about it, I feel...almost happy. Like I can finally breathe again." Her voice dropped a bitter note lower. "But then after that one short breath, it's like I'm drowning all over again. I go to school and see my friends laughing and talking about stuff like what awesome things they want to do when they grow up... Normal teen stuff. I see them sitting there not worrying about anything really—something I never get to do. And when I see that, I get so jealous and sad and angry. And I just *can't breathe*."

Brian's hand gripped the handrail tighter to avoid reaching for her.

A frustrated strength began vibrating through in her words. "I know everyone thinks it's better for me not to take the gene test, and I understand why. If it comes back positive, all that tells me is that I'm going to get HD one day, and that's it; that's all it'll tell me. Not when, not how. So I get it. Everyone's worried that I'm going to get all depressed and give up. Or that I'm going to get all stupid with my life because I think I'm going to die anyway." A shudder wobbled her voice. "But what everyone *doesn't get* is that not knowing makes me feel all of that anyway and more. I feel like I'm not getting to...I dunno, accept it. Or deal with it."

Skylar paused, blinking in thought as if trying to find the right words. At Tessa's encouraging nod, she turned to face him fully. "Okay, dad, pretend...pretend that an awful killer who knew all of your biggest nightmares was chasing you, and you were trapped, with no chance of getting away. And he told you all these horrible things he was going to do to make you suffer a long and slow death...and that he was going to start right away. Like tomorrow." Her voice crackled on a broken cry as she bit out, "Now pretend he didn't do it tomorrow. But he let you go for another day just so he could chase you, trap you, and tell you all those scary things all over again. Then again. And again."

Oh, dear God.

"That's what I feel every day. And I can't ever stop being afraid because every day I wake up and it starts all over again. I wonder, I get angry, I get scared, and I just. Can't. Breathe."

He caught her as she crumpled down to her knees and cried in earnest now. Wrapping his arms around her, he held her as her tears ran without end, as the terrifying descriptions of what she'd been holding inside slashed thousands of knife wounds across his chest, flayed it wide open. "We'll get you through this, Sky-bug," he whispered against her hair. "We'll do whatever we have to so you don't feel like this anymore."

How he was going to make good on that, he had no idea.

⚜

AFTER WITNESSING what had happened with Skylar, and what Brian had gone through seeing his little girl in that kind of pain, Tessa knew it was finally the beginning of the end.

Looking at her bookshelf, she thought about the one Brian had in his house—chock-full of once-in-a-lifetime experiences, happy candids, treasured mementos and souvenirs. While her own lack of memories and keepsakes was a reminder of all she'd never had, his abundance of them reminded her of all he'd once had and then lost.

So much loss already.

Opening her file cabinet, she pulled out a copy of an article that would be getting published in a few months, one she felt strongly about, regarding an important issue she'd been involved in and spreading awareness about since she'd discovered her voice in the silence.

-- PREDICTIVE GENETIC TESTING FOR EARLY TEENS --

Even if it would combat everything Brian believed to be true and best for Skylar, even if it would pain her to have him read it. Even *when*, not if, it would likely damage their relationship irrevocably, she had to help him, help Skylar.

She scanned the article and highlighted the sections she needed Brian to read, before sliding it into a manila envelope with the program pamphlets and other information she'd put together for both Brian and Skylar to read. Grabbing her keys and her bags, she quickly loaded her trunk and left for Brian's house before she could talk herself out of it.

He only lived a few minutes away. For years, they'd been so close and yet a lifetime apart. Still were. Still would be. It was a reality they just couldn't avoid, it seemed.

The door opened before she even stepped foot on the porch, and the smile Brian gave her was one she knew she'd hold on to, even if she couldn't put it on her shelf. The way he looked at her would always be one of her most treasured keepsakes, her most prized memory of all she'd once had.

And lost.

"Hey, I have that article and the other information I was telling you about."

"You're a lifesaver. I've been talking with a few genetic counselors and scouring the internet but the majority still keep citing fifteen as the absolute youngest age to have the gene testing done. Even then, most say it's ill-advised."

And that was definitely a valid, medically sound point of view. Still, she had her own thoughts on the matter. "Here you go." She handed him the envelope. "The highlighted article is just for you. It's different from most of the literature out there. And with it, I've also included some pamphlets for programs I've been working with that I think Skylar should go to so she can meet with folks of all ages living with HD. And I've included the number of the outreach director for several care homes that specialize in Huntington's patients—the one in Cactus Creek included. They'll all be able to arrange visits, and set up meetings with teens and adults who've done the gene test as teens, along with their families. These are folks I know and trust."

Brian looked overwhelmed. "The doctors and counselors didn't even mention a third of this. Have you talked to Skylar about these already?"

"Some of it. But now that she's talked to you about really pursuing the testing, it's time. I've seen cases where the simple act of talking to these people has helped tremendously. Sometimes, just the added knowledge was what they needed to stop feeling like a powerless victim. A lot of times, that's precisely why some individuals take the test, because they're looking for control in an otherwise uncontrollable situation, over an undetermined fate."

He dragged her in close for a hug. "Thank you. For all of this, and for just being there. For being you."

She closed her eyes and breathed him in, not wanting to let go.

But she eventually had to. "I better get going. I'm heading out to the airport now."

"Already? I thought you weren't leaving for your trip until tomorrow."

"I changed my flight plans. I'm going up a day ahead of Connor to get everything set up."

"I'm going to have to talk to my brother about his making you travel so much," he teased, looking like he was missing her already.

She was too.

"At least let me give you a proper goodbye kiss."

He leaned in and kissed her gently, but thoroughly. Like he had all the time in the world, but none of the restraint. She loved that about his kisses. They always went straight to her head. Her heart.

"So I'll see you the night you get back?"

She had to get out of there before she caved. "I'm not sure yet."

"Okay, well that weekend then?"

Sliding into her car, she said lightly, "No making plans further than a week out, remember?" She closed the door before he could reply and started the engine, rolling down the window for one final goodbye as she shifted the car into reverse. "I'll call you. In the meantime, read the literature. Start with the article. And make sure you and Skylar go through the packet to see which ones she might want to do."

"Tessa—"

"Call me if you need to talk about...anything. I might not be able to answer. But I promise, if you leave a message, I'll listen to it and call you back when I can."

Then she reversed out of his driveway as quickly as she could.

***

AS HE WATCHED HER speed off down his street, Brian felt everything male inside of him clamoring to chase after her. Something about her parting statement sounded...off. And not Tessa-off. Just off in general. Brian couldn't put his finger on it. Could be that he was just grouchy over her joke about not making plans. The reminder of her 'fling rules' had him growling. She couldn't possibly think this was still just a fling between them, could she?

Because it sure as hell was more for him.

Spreading out all the materials on the coffee table, he picked up the article she'd mentioned first. He only had another ten minutes or so before Skylar got home from the movies so he started skimming the parts Tessa had highlighted for him just so he could have some food for thought while he got dinner ready.

History: Subject was thirteen years old when her gene test came back positive. Soon after, her life began spiraling out of control. With little regard for her safety, Subject began a self-destructive stretch that lasted until high school.

Shit. This was exactly what he was worried about. This is why he hated case studies. He pictured Skylar going through every described case and it about killed him.

Subject had been forced by her mother to take the gene test against her wishes. Subject was not given the proper time, information, or support to prepare or process after the fact. When the results came back, Subject noted: "While I felt like I'd just gotten a death sentence, my mother treated it like she'd been sentenced to life without parole because she'd have to take care of me."

Jesus Christ, the mother sounded like a monster.

Subject asserted that the absence of preparation, support, and choice was the determining factor that resulted in as much resentment of the test itself, which was compounded by the results. The lack of choice made Subject feel more helpless over her situation, and betrayed by those whose support is vital during the gene testing.

Put in the same situation, he'd undoubtedly feel the same way.

> *Subject's downward spiral came to an end when she hit what she deemed to be rock bottom. From there, she identified two factors that helped turn her life around: 1) the return of control over her decisions, short-term goals, and future, and 2) her positive relationships with other individuals living with HD.*

That was promising. Hence all of Tessa's pamphlets and programs.

> *Longitudinal follow-up: Subject is now living a productive life. In her experience now as an adult who underwent predictive testing as an early teen, Subject has found one major area where the knowledge of her gene test result has seemed irreversibly detrimental: in her relationships with a significant other.*

Brian's eyes narrowed on that last tidbit and a sudden feeling of unease hit him.

> *Had she not been aware of her having the HD gene, Subject feels that she would be able to love and receive love more freely in a relationship. But because she is aware, Subject is unwilling to put a significant other through what her mother treated as "a life sentence without parole."*

Fear and dread gripped him in the throat as he flipped through the pages to the final highlighted section, somehow knowing it held something he didn't want to know, couldn't bear to see in black and white.

It wasn't a page from the article.

It was an anonymity waiver.

Subject Name: Tessa Daniels

A dark wave of cruel, harsh reality slammed into him.

Tessa had the HD gene.

Why the thought had never even occurred to him was beyond him. He knew the data. The chances of inheriting the HD gene were always exactly 50-50. For some reason, with Willow having had the juvenile form, he hadn't even thought twice about Tessa having the gene as well. But she did have it. And as was the case for every person with the gene, that meant she'd develop the disease at some point in her life.

The air in his lungs burned suddenly and he felt like someone was reaching in and ripping out his heart.

Again.

But more than that, he felt his heart breaking for Tessa. For everything she'd gone through, everything she was going through. Everything she'd be going through in the future.

Picking up his phone, he dialed her number and got her voicemail. Listening to her sweet, cheerful voice, he was at a loss for words. What could he say to the woman who thought his loving her would be a life sentence without parole for him?

With no answer to that question, he hung up before the beep.

CHAPTER TEN

"Brian, can you stay and color with me?"

Tessa came to a jarring halt out in the hallway just outside of Jilly's room, the mere mention of Brian's name sending her insides into an emotional tailspin.

She'd gotten back from her trip almost a week ago, and she hadn't been able to return Brian's call yet. What could she say to the man who now knew that her future would be an instant replay of the nightmares in his past?

To be honest, she'd *almost* called him back during the trip after hearing his message. About a dozen times. But it had taken only a single glance at Connor's face to know that he'd talked to Brian...one glance to know exactly what he thought about his brother going through that nightmare again.

She couldn't blame him.

So here she was, hiding, and seemingly unable to drag herself away from the chance to see Brian. When he turned to smile his adoring, thousand-watt smile at Jilly, Tessa felt the air in her lungs vanish. And just like that, the longstanding fortress she'd managed to resurrect around her heart over the past week and a half crumbled.

Tessa had first brought Brian to meet Jilly a few weeks back. And of course, Jilly had him wrapped around her little finger within the first five minutes.

Impressively, Jilly had sweet-talked him into volunteering to build a birdhouse for her by minute six. A quick peek at the far window revealed that he had in fact finished the birdhouse for Jilly. And it was beautiful.

He was such a good man.

Her head resting against the door, her heart scattered all over the place, Tessa just stood there in the hall and watched Brian grab the crayon bucket and sit with Jilly.

"So what are we going to color today, Angel-face?"

"I got a new coloring book last week. See?"

"*Flintstones?*" he chuckled, his eyes softening. "Let me guess, Tessa got this one for you."

Tessa nearly fell apart right then and there. Those teal blue eyes of his had looked as filled with pain as hers did when she looked in the mirror lately.

Jilly beamed. "We watched it on TV once. It's so *funny*! The people drive their cars with their feet and they have birds in their cameras." She shook her head to herself with a giggling sigh as she started coloring in Pebbles.

Brian's voice shifted into what Tessa liked to call his 'super dad mode' as he picked up a purple crayon to start coloring in Dino. "Say, do you think this Dino dinosaur and Barney are related? They're both purple. Maybe they're cousins or something."

Tessa bit her lip as she listened in. Once, she'd watched Brian incite the most outlandish conversation with his colleague's three-year-old son in the supermarket check-out line. It had gone on for at least five minutes.

"Dino and Barney can't be cousins!" Jilly gaped at him as if he were the silliest person alive. "Dino is from the *olden* days. Barney is from right-now times."

After visibly smothering a smile when she said 'olden days,' he continued on with impressively straight-faced stamina. "Get out! We still have dinosaurs in right-now times? Are they purple like Barney? Are they friendly? Where do they *live?*"

Jilly splayed both her hands over her eyes and fell back against the bed dramatically. "Oh my goodness, you make me tired."

Brian tipped his head back and chortled over that one as he leaned over and pulled her into a gentle hug. "You are just the cutest thing in the world, Angel-face."

The entire verbal volleyball match was the tipping point for Tessa. She had to get out of there. Her heart couldn't take much more.

Just as she turned to leave, however, Jilly's gaze swung over in her direction.

"*Tessa!* Look, Brian. Tessa's here!"

Brian's head shot up and he stared at her for a raw second as if he just couldn't help it. Then he came over quickly to explain, "I was just dropping off Jilly's birdhouse." He lowered his voice. "I wasn't trying to corner you or anything, I swear. I know you said you'd call me back when you're ready to talk…"

The trailing pause killed her. Because honestly, she didn't think she'd ever be ready.

"I'll go," he said softly.

Tessa backed up a step. "No, no. You stay. I can go."

"Why can't you *both* stay?" asked Jilly, brows furrowed with all the candidness of a six-year-old.

Why indeed.

"I wanted to show you guys what I did in art class this week."

Brian looked over at Tessa with a silent *'It's your call.'*

"Sure, Jilly-bean," replied Tessa. "Of course we'll both stay and look at what you made."

"Yaay!"

Not long after, the tension had dissipated considerably, thanks largely to Jilly's hilarious works of art, which Tessa was pinning up for her on the 'masterpiece clothes line' while Brian and Jilly were busy discussing the finer aspects of art like a pair of hardcore aficionados.

"You kidding?" he was telling Jilly. "You can do way more things with watercolor painting than finger painting."

"Nuh-uh!"

"Uh-huh," he mimicked with a grin. "Skylar and I used to do all sorts of cool watercolor projects. Hell, she still—"

Jilly gasped. "You cursed!"

Brian froze and shot Tessa a stricken look.

Even though humor was the last thing she was feeling,

Tessa managed to chuckle. "Jilly's yanking your chain. Her mom swears worse than a gold-toothed rapper"

Jilly's little legs flutter-kicked under the blanket as she giggled with delight. "I got you! I got you!" she sang out between laughing screeches when Brian got his tickle-monster claws up and started faking left and going right.

"Ah, so *this* is where all the cackling is coming from," teased Nurse Liv as she entered the room to do a routine check and update Jilly's charts. "Sorry to break up the party, but I've got to get this little girl ready for her PT session."

Brian got out of her way and joined Tessa by the activity shelf to help clean up.

"Oh! I almost forgot," Jilly bubbled from across the room. "I'm gonna get to go in the pool again today."

"Yep." Liv got a comb and started braiding Jilly's hair. "According to your physical therapist, you're getting to be quite the little mermaid, sweetie."

"I might even be able to go in with just the floaties at the next pool party." Jilly did a little wiggly dance and then called out around Liv, "I asked my mommy if she could get grown-up floaties for you, Tessa. That way you can come in the water too this time."

Brian turned a questioning gaze her way as Jilly asked Liv what sort of game booths the nurses would be doing at this next party.

"Floaties?" he asked quietly, but not at all meanly.

Tessa responded with a shrugging smile. "I never got the chance to learn how to swim."

His mouth turned down at the corners as empathy warmed his gaze, and she just knew he was about to say something undoubtedly sweet...so she broke the connection and cut him off at the pass. "So how are things going with Skylar? She hasn't skyped me since last week, but she sounded pretty upbeat when she did."

"She's been doing a lot better, actually," he replied, looking thrown by the conversational one-eighty, though he covered it up well. "Those visits you recommended have really helped. She's been flat-out inspired by those kids and she's starting to get passionate about a lot of the projects. Just yesterday, she asked if there were things she could do to help out."

"That's fantastic." Tessa felt herself smiling her first real smile of the day. "I'm glad."

He took a step closer and his eyes ran over her face slowly, as if cherishing each detail. "I've missed you so much, Tessa. Could we just—"

"I'm sorry I didn't tell you about my having HD sooner," she blurted out quietly, lowering her voice so Liv and Jilly couldn't overhear. "It's not exactly something I advertise...but I should've told you. Before we..."

What? Had sex?

Became more than flinger and flingee?

He sighed raggedly. "Honestly, I understand why you didn't, but I really wish you would've. You don't always have to take on the weight of the world alone, you know."

Oh yes, she did. She was *not* going to be her mother.

"You may not have had the support system you needed then, but you have it now." He reached for her hand. "Please, let's talk about this."

No. She couldn't.

She couldn't allow him to be that guy. The one who could easily become everything she'd never dreamed possible for her life. The one who *would* be and do all that and more, even though he'd already gone through this once before.

She simply couldn't allow it.

Because he was already the man she loved so much, she was willing to walk away.

Backing up a step, she tried to put it all into words. "Brian, I just don't think—"

Liv's voice interrupted her thoughts, "Okay, Jilly, you can visit with Tessa and Brian for another ten minutes and then I'll be back to get you changed, you hear?"

When she saw Liv's crystalline gaze slide covertly over to Brian again while Jilly called him over to show him the recent swim strokes she'd learned, Tessa felt a knife blade of jealousy slash through her. Followed by a harsh dose of reality.

That's the kind of woman who'd be perfect for Brian.

Watching as Liv headed back over to the computer at the nurse's station, Tessa cataloged all the stark differences between them. Though they were the same age, Liv was chic and classy, and she always had it together. Tessa was none of these things.

In the looks department, ironically, Liv was a pretty remarkable cross between Beth and Abby. Meanwhile, Tessa looked like a cross between a modern hippy and an urban gypsy. Proudly. But still.

Glancing up at her reflection on the wall opposite her, Tessa noted all the contrasts like a glaring pro and con list. With her candy apple red-tipped hair this week and her *Popeye the Sailor Man* shirt, she was no match for Liv.

Echoes of her conversation with her mom reverberated in her brain. *He deserves better.*

Yep, Liv would most definitely be that 'better.'

Tessa came to a decision then, her feet already carrying her across the room before she lost her nerve…or her lunch.

"Brian, you stay. I need to get to a meeting." She blew Jilly a giant kiss. "See you in a few days, Jilly-bean. I'll bring a new video game for us next time, okay?"

Avoiding Brian's intense gaze, Tessa gave him a quick, friendly wave as well and left the room. As she headed to the nurse's station, she felt a thousand needles piercing her heart with each step she took. Which was nothing compared to the almost unbearable nausea that hit her when she started chatting up Liv…about Brian.

And still, when she left shortly after and heard Liv call out to Brian as he was leaving Jilly's room, somehow Tessa found the strength to keep on walking.

~~~

OF ALL THE INFURIATING…

Tessa had set him up on a date with *another woman*.

Unbelievable.

Instead of letting him prove to her that her having the HD gene wouldn't affect their relationship, she'd gone and convinced Nurse Liv to ask him out.

It didn't matter that he knew she was trying to do what she thought was best for him.

He was still pissed.

Because if she'd just pick up her damn phone and call him, she'd know that her conclusions on the situation were just plain wrong. The fact that he'd gone through all this once before with Beth wasn't sending him screaming in the other direction from Tessa. Maybe some would run, but not him. He'd never go back and erase his time with Beth and Skylar, regardless of how difficult the latter half of their marriage had been. Absolutely not. Everyone reduced his marriage to Beth to her last years, her toughest ones, but he chose to remember all the others. None of the horrible challenges her disease put them both through could or would ever negate the good of their shared life together.

The same would hold true with Tessa. Of that, he had no doubt. It didn't matter if her HD symptoms started tomorrow; he still wouldn't choose *not* to be with her. Moreover, the thought of Tessa going through this *without him* one day made him...rabid. Alpha protectiveness was a mild description of what feelings that inspired.

Now, if Brian weren't having the world's most awkward conversation with Liv at the moment, it was very likely he'd be chucking his brilliant let-Tessa-come-to-him plan in lieu of heading to Tessa's apartment right now and banging down the door so he could—

What? He sighed. What could he do? Tell her that her feelings were unwarranted, that her methods of dealing with all of this were just plain crazy?

That wouldn't help his cause one bit.

He just couldn't believe that *this* was Tessa's big solution. To set him up with Liv—who was amazingly still talking. He smiled at her, and she smiled back, ecstatic. Okay, so she was pretty and very nice—reminded him a bit of Beth, in fact. Was that what it was? He tried to see her from Tessa's eyes, to see whatever it was that she thought was better for him than she'd ever be. Liv was beautiful, yes. Seemingly uncomplicated so far, sure. And…well, *normal.*

After spending all this time with Tessa, he wasn't sure what 'normal' was anymore, or if that was even what he wanted. Used to be. But now…

He knew what he had to do.

Preparing himself to head into completely unchartered territory, he put his hand on Liv's shoulder to put an end to her nervous rambling and asked, "Do you want to get out here? Maybe grab a bite at a quiet restaurant where we can talk?"

Liv smiled—not a rainbow-eyed smile, but a sweet, pretty smile nonetheless.

"I'd like that."

Here goes nothing.

CHAPTER ELEVEN

IT WAS THREE WEEKS to the day. Three weeks since Tessa had seen Brian last. Three weeks since she'd overheard Liv gush to her nurse friends out in the hall about how happy she was to have met such a great guy.

Three weeks since Tessa had laughed.

Because every minute of those three weeks had hurt.

Tessa had avoided Liv like the plague since the day she'd set her up with Brian. It didn't take a genius to see that she'd been right about that particular match. Liv was a great woman, a wonderful nurse to Jilly, and a sweet person all around. All personal feelings aside, Tessa really was genuinely happy for her. And for Brian as well. He was an incredible man, an amazing father to Skylar, and a real-deal good guy who deserved the best. In her heart of hearts, she knew she'd done right by him by cutting things off like her mom had suggested.

But *still*, it hurt.

And though she'd been able to plaster a smile on her face the few times she had run into Connor or Abby, or during her weekly skype chats with Skylar, she *knew* she wouldn't be able to keep up the charade around Liv. Definitely not around Brian, either.

Which was why they were now going on three weeks to the day of her avoiding them both.

And still, it *hurt*.

"Hey Tessa!"

Damn it, damn it, damn it. Tessa dug deep and slapped the best impression of a smile she could on her face before she turned around. "Hey Liv. How's everything going?"

Liv lit up like a Christmas tree. "So incredible. The past few weeks have been...oh my gosh, I can't even describe it."

Oh good. Please don't.

"I've never been so happy."

"That's wonderful, Liv. I'm glad it's all working out so well." She was going to have to wash that last one down with some tequila later. Because right now, it was burning a jagged hole through her stomach.

And her heart.

Even though looking at Liv in all her joyful radiance was a bit like jabbing hot toothpicks into her eyes, she still appreciated what was standing there before her.

Love.

Lucky girl.

Liv gripped her arm. *What do you know, hot toothpicks on skin hurt like a bitch too.* "So Tessa, I really wanted to do something for you as a thank-you. I mean, if it weren't for what you did, I wouldn't have ended up meeting the man of my dreams."

Okay, let's not get carried away. It was only three weeks to the day.

"My mom just loves him. And I absolutely adore his mother," continued Liv, practically floating down the hall as they talked.

Well, hell. Tessa had met Brian's mother as well, but that was only via Connor. But then again, why *would* Brian have introduced the girl he was having a casual fling with to his mother?

He wouldn't. Those kind of introductions were reserved for...

Tessa stopped that train of thought before it crashed into the conclusion of what his introducing Liv to his mother meant.

Geez, was she still talking?

"...And we're going away for a week-long vacation next month."

Ouch. Now that one really hurt. Time to jump off this sinking ship and into the welcome shark-infested waters. "Hey, sorry Liv, but I really have to run. We'll catch up more some other time, okay?"

"Wait, don't go yet. I actually wanted to know if you were free tomorrow for lunch. There's going to be a concert at Ocotillos."

"Oh no, that's okay. I'm not much of a dancer."

"Well then just go to have lunch. You have to. You did this amazing thing by setting me up with someone you thought was perfect for me. Now let me repay the favor. I have a good friend who I think is *perfect* for you."

"What? Oh no, that's *really* not necessary. Thank you, but I'm not into blind dates."

"I'm not going to take no for an answer, Tessa. You're beautiful and just plain awesome. You deserve to be with a great guy. Besides, it's just one innocent meal." Liv crossed her arms and gave her the 'nurse' look that she used on prickly patients.

Damn, the woman was persistent. "Errr...I guess if it's just lunch."

"Great! We'll meet you at eleven tomorrow outside of Ocotillos."

"Wait, *we*?"

"Yes! It's a double date. It'll be fun!"

"But—"

"Oh! My break is over. Gotta run. See you tomorrow!"

And then she was off.

Tessa fell back against the wall and rapped the back of her head against it, once, twice, and then a third time just because.

A double date with Mr. and Mrs. Perfect.

This was going to be an absolute nightmare.

⁓≈⁓

"HEY TESSA. You look great. How've you been?"

Awful, miserable, heartbroken. "Good," she lied with the

smile she'd practiced in front of the mirror for the last hour. "You look good too, Brian. Where's Liv?"

"She's inside getting a drink. I told her I'd stay out here and wait for you."

Always the nice guy.

"Thanks. You want to head in?"

Tessa almost fell flat on her face when she felt Brian's hand ghost across her back.

"You okay, sweetheart?"

The endearment was a knife to her gut. "I'm fine. Where'd you say Liv was?" The faster she could get through this lunch, the better.

"The concert's on the rooftop. We have a table on the side opposite the dance floor."

Tessa knew the way, so she hotwheeled it over to the stairwell, leaving Brian in her dust. The last thing she needed was him coming up from behind her on the stairwell.

When she got to the roof deck, she looked around.

"Our table's over in the corner," came Brian's voice, right next to her ear.

Dammit. She couldn't stop the shiver that ran through her system.

How long would his voice have this effect on her?

Forever, probably.

Brian pointed over to a booth with a reserved tag on it, and waited for her to slide in...before he slid in right after her, effectively trapping her in there.

This day just kept getting better and better.

Tessa scanned the crowd, finally seeing Liv on the dance floor, dancing with a pretty handsome guy.

"So is that my date?" she asked, acutely aware of how close Brian was sitting to her.

"What?" he asked in her ear.

Why in the world was the music so loud in this place?

"I asked if that guy Liv's dancing with is my date."

"No," he rumbled across her jawline. "That's *her* date."

Momentarily drunk off the feel of his lips skimming across her cheek, it took a while for his words to register.

Even then, it didn't make a lick of sense.

When she stared at him, mouth agape with confusion, he smiled. "I think this is the first time I've managed to give you back one of your token nonsensical answers."

He moved in closer and said, "Tell me the truth, please. Have you missed me as much as I've missed you, sweetheart?"

Suddenly, the music wasn't too loud anymore.

His words were ringing through clear as a bell, their only competition being the pounding of her heart.

"Yes," she replied truthfully.

His smile just about knocked her into tomorrow. "Good." He brushed a soft kiss against her lips, before taking her hand in his. "Then come on, I'll introduce you to Liv's date so we can get started on ours."

⁂

HE COULDN'T get her out of the restaurant fast enough.

After spending exactly one minute making introductory

small talk with Liv and her date, Brian had ushered Tessa out of Ocotillos and into his SUV, promising simply that he'd drive her back later to get her car.

Then he took the long way around the car to get himself under control.

Three goddamn weeks since he'd seen her last. Three goddamn weeks since she *gave up* on them and tried to fix him up with someone else. Three goddamn weeks since he'd held the woman he was in love with in his arms.

And every second since had hurt like hell.

He'd been up front with Liv from the very beginning. They'd had a nice dinner, during which, he'd poured his heart out about Tessa, and Liv had poured her heart out about the man she'd been hopelessly in love with for two years.

Her problem was about a thousand times easier.

So they'd tackled hers first. One call and she'd had herself a date—seriously, why did some women have to make the whole thing so difficult? Guys were simple beings, really. Sometimes too simple. The complicated workings of the female mind involving subtle signals over the course of two years was, nine times out of ten, way too difficult for the average guy's brain to comprehend. A call asking him out, however...ding-ding-ding. Simple.

That's when they moved on to Brian's problem.

A much bigger problem with a far more complex female mind, the likes of which, he'd been lost without a compass and a map trying to figure out. So he'd called a full deployment, gathering Connor, Abby, Skylar, his mother, and

Liv together to devise a plan.

He'd hated their plan from the start.

They'd told him to give her time to sort through her feelings—two to three weeks minimum—and he'd nearly walked out right then, with every intention of just stomping over to Tessa's apartment and throwing her over his shoulder to drag her back to his cave. But they'd worn him down eventually. And he ended up spending the next three weeks miserable as all hell following their plan to the tee.

At least it looked like it'd been worth it.

The way she'd responded to his lips on her skin earlier...

His hands gripped the steering wheel tighter.

The woman was still an expert at zapping his control. Before getting ahead of himself and hoping for more than he ought to at this point, he launched into the explanation her bamboozled, utterly confounded, but thankfully unshuttered expression was patiently requesting.

Ten minutes later, she was still gaping at him.

"So the man that Liv is all gaga over is the guy she was with today."

"Yup."

"And the last three weeks—"

"Have been unmitigated torture for me," he broke in.

Silence.

"For me, too," she said quietly.

He frowned. "I didn't want it to be that hard for you. Honest. That's the part of their plan I hated the most. That was why I asked Skylar, Connor, and Abby to keep you company when they could."

Startled, she gave him a small grin. "I *thought* they'd been a little clingy these past few weeks." Her voice got watery. "I can't believe you did that for me, even though you were going through the same thing."

He shrugged. "I didn't want you to be sad and lonely the entire time. You've had enough of that in your life."

Giving him a look he couldn't quite decipher, she said softly, "Thank you. Not just for trying to spare me that, but for giving me time as well."

He didn't want to push, so he didn't ask what the results of all her time thinking and sorting had led her to. He was just happy she was there with him now.

"Listen, Brian—"

"Nope. No big relationship conversations yet. Please." Just in case she still didn't want to be with him, he still wanted her to have this day. "I have a surprise for you first. We'll talk after, I promise. Deal?"

After a long beat, she nodded. "Deal." As they got farther and farther from the city, she peered out at the passing streets. "Where exactly are we going?"

"I told you, it's a surprise. Actually, cover your eyes. No peeking."

A minute later, he parked and helped her out of the car door, placing his hands over her eyes so she could use hers to balance. "I know the ground is a little rough. Just keep walking straight, about ten more steps."

She tilted her head a bit and sniffed the air. "Are we at a

lumberyard?" she asked, her voice brimming with adorable anticipation. He wondered then if Tessa had ever had anyone surprise her with a gift. From all accounts of her past, it seemed unlikely.

He stopped and pulled his hands off her eyes. "Okay, you can look now."

Blinking rapidly to take the scene before her in, she absorbed every square inch of the deserted lot behind the lumberyard her dad had worked at, which had been transformed to now include strategically placed piles of dirt and gravel, some shallow trenches, a few small boulders, and the equivalent of mini 'speed bumps' and winding pathways with traffic cones.

Just as he'd envisioned for weeks.

The more she took in, the more her curious smile just grew and grew.

When the star of the show—a big yellow construction vehicle—pulled up and stopped dead-center in the lot, she spun back around. "Is that Frank driving?"

"Yep. He and I spent the past few days putting together this little obstacle course for you."

"Obstacle course?" She turned back to survey the lot with a whole new light in her eyes.

"That's right," called out Frank, walking over. "Your gentleman friend here tracked me down and came up with this little surprise for you. He was here at the butt-crack of dawn with me clearing this side of the lot out and getting all this set up." He pointed back at the construction vehicle. "My only condition on you riding the backhoe loader was that I be the one to teach you how to handle it, for safety reasons."

Her eyes widened with delight. "You mean I'm going to drive *that* through the obstacle course?"

"Not just drive it, dollface, you're going to be operating it. Brian here's made a few little challenges for you that you need to use the digger and the shovel for. It'll give me a chance to see if you inherited any of your dad's genes." Frank winked. "Because let me tell you, your old man was great with the equipment but, god rest him, he drove like shit."

Tessa burst out laughing and wrapped Frank up in a giant hug. "That's why I always used to drive us everywhere."

He ruffled her hair lightly. "Then there's hope for you yet. So come on now, let's get cracking."

"I'll be right there. Just give me a minute to talk with Brian first."

"Alright, but keep it PG-13 you hear? It's not like the boy bought you a ring or nothing. No need to be thanking him all that hard."

Embarrassed shock flooded her expression. "Frank!"

"What? I'm just saying. Wouldn't want to have to get your friend acquainted with the business end of my shotgun after all the hard work he put in this morning."

A deep blush tinted her cheeks as she hollered again, "Frank!"

"I'll be over there if you need me."

Tessa shook her head in disbelief. "I don't know what's gotten into him."

"Can't blame the man for watching out for you." Brian chuckled, brushing his knuckles over her flushed cheeks. "You're like the daughter he never had."

Reaching into his backseat, Brian produced a small hardhat along with a pair of socks and sneakers in her size. "With actual backs to them," he added with a pointed look at her backless sneakers.

She giggled softly.

"So do you like your surprise so far?"

She cupped his face in her hands. "I *love* it. Thank you." The kiss she brushed against his lips was soft, just barely edging over the line of friendship. "But I thought you said this was a date. I thought we'd get to do something together. I really have missed you."

He growled and pulled her back in for another kiss...which was not at all soft, with his foot way the hell over that friendship line. But he kept it short. He'd never actually seen the business end of a shotgun and didn't have any desire to.

Rubbing his thumb across her lower lip, he commented lightly, "Can't say I ever kissed someone in a hardhat before. I gotta tell you, it's a little weird."

Her eyes danced. "Now you're starting to sound like me. I think I'm rubbing off on you."

"Woman, keep talking like that and that shotgun will be here before I know it."

This time her chuckle was laced with a touch of heat.

A loud, warbly throat-clearing from across the lot

effectively put a buzz kill on that.

"I think our time's up." He gave her one last kiss. "And by the way, this surprise was just for you. Our part's after. But I wanted you to have this regardless. I remember you telling me how your dad used to be so happy doing this, even after his HD symptoms started setting in."

She nodded, eyes watering.

"I just wanted to give you back a little of that happiness."

CHAPTER TWELVE

AN HOUR LATER, Brian still couldn't take his eyes off Tessa's face. Watching her go through the obstacle course was like watching a child experience her first miracle.

The way she was smiling now was unlike any smile he'd seen from her yet. It was priceless. She was having the time of her life out there gouging out holes in the dirt and shoveling up branches and rocks. As an added bonus, this was the slowest he'd ever seen her drive, so that was also a nice miracle to observe in action.

As she passed the three-quarter mark of the obstacle course, Frank joined him, looking like a proud papa as he watched Tessa clear her last pile of debris before making her way over to the trench she had to roll over and extend about ten feet. "I meant what I said earlier, you know."

"About the shotgun?" Brian smiled. "I know."

"Well, that too. But mostly about the ring. Tessa mentioned you two just started getting friendly a couple of months ago. That may not seem long to you, but take it from me, when you know, you know."

He actually wholeheartedly agreed.

"Any man who would give Tessa-girl a construction vehicle obstacle course instead of a dozen roses is a man who should be getting down on one knee if you ask me. God knows that girl deserves some happiness." A flash of pain etched across his features. "She's been alone for too long. Even as kid, I can't tell you how many times I rushed over to the hospital on account of Willow. Each time, I'd see Tessa just sitting out in the hall all by herself. Damn near watched her grow up in that hall. Used to break my heart."

"Every so many months, I'd see an older version of her sitting in that spot, worrying over her sister and her parents." His jaw clenched in anger then. "And after that flake of a mother stopped being able to cut it, hell, Tessa just stepped in and took care of her sister and daddy both. Never seen anything like it. That kind of grit and heart…you can't fake it, can't even pray for it. But Tessa, she's got it in spades."

Just then, Tessa stopped working the two huge joystick-looking controllers and spun the seat out of operator mode to wave at them, hollering out, "I did it! And in a pretty straight line, too!"

Well. It probably looked straight from where she was standing. Brian laughed and waved back. "Looks great, honey."

After doing a little dance—to which, Frank scolded, "*seatbelt!*"—she spun her into drive mode and proceeded to steer the backhoe loader over the last stretch of dips and mounds on her way to the finish line.

"You better not hurt her, boy. Because I have a lot full of equipment that can guarantee your body never gets found if you do."

A squealing hoot, pounding footsteps on soft dirt, and an airborne hug flying into his arms prevented him from answering.

"Thank you, thank you, thank you!" Tessa was out of breath and absolutely radiant in her happiness. "That was so much fun!"

Shotgun bedamned. Brian pulled her into a python hug and captured her lips to share in some of that joy.

When he finally let her down, he watched her cheeks flush as she turned to look at Frank.

Who was already walking away. "Looks like I don't have anything to worry about. Okay, kids, it's been fun but I need to get home to the missus and whatever fish she's cookin' tonight."

"Wait!" Tessa ran over and gave him another hug. "This was amazing, Frank. Thank you."

Frank looked about as close to emotional as a big, rough construction guy could look. "It's been a while since I've seen this smile, dollface. If your man there is the cause of it, hold on to him. You deserve to be happy."

The quiet, fleeting look of hope on her face gutted Brian wide open.

When she came walking back, bright-eyed smile back in place, Brian pulled her into his arms tight and just held on. "He's right you know. You do deserve to be happy. I don't care what your quack of a mom may have drilled into your head."

She untangled herself from his arms. "Does this mean it's time for our talk now?"

Damn. He hated seeing her smile disappear. "No rush. We can grab dinner first—"

"No. We should talk first." She took a deep breath. "I know you don't think highly of my mom, but you can't say she's completely wrong on this. The only thing I can offer a man long term is heartbreak. And in your case, it's so much worse. You already had one HD wife. I can't sentence you to having another."

His heart stopped. "Are you saying you've thought about being my wife someday?" Saying it out loud made his heart restart at triple its original rate.

She looked stunned, but quickly stuttered back with, "Seriously? *That's* your only takeaway from everything I just said?"

"No, I also heard what sounded like—no offense—absolute crap."

At her astonished glare, he bulldozed right along. "You're so much more than your disease and you know it. Heartbreak doesn't scare me. Being without you does."

Her soft gasp had hope surging through his veins.

The truth of the matter was that Tessa inspired him. She made him want to do more than just survive love; she made him want to make the most of it, continue hoping for it when it seemed all but lost.

That's why they belonged together.

In so many ways, they were as different as night and day. Folks used to say that while he and Beth were like two peas in a pod, he and Abby were like the same pea split in half.

Now he and Tessa, on the other hand... Hell, they were like two different vegetables altogether. And he wouldn't have it any other way.

"No one's okay with heartbreak," she argued back, bringing him out of his own head. "Can you honestly say you didn't think for even a moment when you found out I had the HD gene that the universe was giving you a lightning strike for the second time in your life?" she demanded.

"No, I can't. Because you're right, I did think it. But that's my point. I *have* been through the very thing you're afraid of. I'm not being idealistic here. I know it's going to be hard. But I love you, Tessa. You make me love harder and with less restraint than even I thought possible. And now, I just can't imagine my life or my future any other way."

Emotions fully charged now, he asked finally because he just had to know, "If the positions were reversed, Tessa, would you stay with me?"

"In a heartbeat," she whispered without hesitation. "Til your very last heartbeat."

When he eventually managed to get air back into his lungs after that fierce declaration, he asked simply, "Then why the hell aren't we together?"

The answer surprised even him.

"Because I'm scared." She bit her lip. "I'm scared, and

for so many years now, there's been no one in my life to care whether I was scared or not. It's kind of like that tree in the woods that no one would hear fall. No one cared before that I had HD, and I'd built my life around that. Being that tree in the woods made it all easier. But now…now, I care that you care. I care that you know just how terrified I am. Not just about how that damn disease is going to steal my body, but how terrified I am that it's going to slowly steal you away from me too. The thought that one day, I might not remember your name, your face, an entire lifetime with you…scares me so much I can't even bear the thought." The last came out on a broken whisper.

His hands speared through her hair with an almost bruising force before he admitted quietly, "I know, sweetheart. I'm terrified of that too—for you, and for me. Even thinking about it kills me every time."

"Then why put yourself through that nightmare a second time? I wouldn't wish how I'm feeling on anyone, let alone someone I love…" Her voice cracked, faded. And though she didn't say it, her expression screamed at the top of her lungs: *How can you honestly think I'm worth it?*

He stared into her eyes and shook his head. "You don't get it do you? Every nightmare I've had since you told me about your HD gene test hasn't been about the tough future ahead for us—it's been picturing us apart. The thought of you facing this alone breaks my heart, and the thought of my life without you just plain rips out my soul. I've only just found you and I can't bear the thought of losing you. You're not getting rid of me. So please say you'll give us a chance. And please say it now because I really don't think I can take another minute apart."

When she just stood there, looking at him with tears in her eyes, he kicked himself for pushing. It was too much, too soon. He'd scared her off—

"I can't bear the thought of losing you either."

"Thank God." His mouth went slamming down onto hers, and he all but lost it when she began kissing him back with the same raw urgency.

It took a while, but eventually he remembered that they were out in public with a trigger-happy father figure to Tessa not far away. So, he grabbed her hand and walked them back to his SUV. "Now, do want me to take you back to your car?"

She shook her head, those wide, witchy eyes of hers—darkened with red-hot longing and half-dazed with arousal—drifted down to his mouth. It was all he could do not to toss her over his shoulder right now.

His heart pounded in his chest. "So where do you want to go instead?"

She turned and climbed into the passenger seat. "My place is closer."

Hot damn.

⊗

They got back to her apartment in record time.

And still, Tessa had very nearly asked him to pull over twice on the way.

Something told her he would've said yes.

Crashing through the door and shedding their clothes on their way to her bedroom, he looked almost predatory as he advanced on her, pure alpha lust rolling off of him in waves.

Though her body was responding in kind, she felt her feet backing up, her breathing going haywire.

Then he smiled. Slow, hot, and sexy. And she swore her panties almost slid off her hips on their own accord.

Her legs eventually bumped into the foot of her bed and she took her eyes off of him for a second to catch her balance. Within that second, he pounced. His lips came down on hers with a hunger that simply fed her own. Her hands slid under the hem of his shirt, and his slid down her body.

"I've been going crazy without you, Tessa," he growled before reaching down and gripping the backs of her thighs in his hands, literally sweeping her off her feet. She fell back onto the bed and felt his body cover hers in a hot rush almost upon impact.

"Just so we're clear. That former contract I signed is now null and void. I'm making love to you in this bed. I'm going to make you come so many times you pass out in exhaustion. And you're going to damn well let me hold you all night as you sleep. Then we're going to spend the next two days doing the exact same thing on every horizontal inch of this apartment—and some vertical ones. Then on Sunday, I'm taking you back home so we can tell Skylar that you and I are serious about each other."

As far as her heart was concerned, the man was a poet.

"So you're planning on breaking every single one of the expert fling rules in one fell swoop?"

He dragged her shirt up off her body and kept her wrists pinned above her head with one hand while sliding up her skirt with the other. "Not only that, but I'm going to enforce some new ones." His teeth raked over her collarbone. "For starters," he kissed his way lower, "you're not allowed to hide how you're feeling from me anymore," he demanded against her skin, his lips closing over and languidly torturing first one nipple. And then the other.

She bit her lip to keep from crying out.

With a heated smile, he tsked and slipped a hand up her inner thigh. "Not even a minute in and you've already broken the first rule." He teased his thumb along the edge of her panties, staring into her eyes. "I don't want just a few romps of sex. I want all of you. Every beautiful imperfection, every odd quirk that I can't seem to get enough of. Your past, present and future—I want you to share it all with me, Tessa."

He brushed over her slick heat and groaned in perfect harmony to her needy gasp.

But then he paused. "Tell me now if that's not what you want, too." Another torturous glide of his thumb. "Not just *this* but all of this, the whole package." A palpable tension steeled his entire frame.

She wriggled her hands free from his hold, slid out from under him and scooted back just a bit.

A dark cloud settled over his features.

"Only if that rule goes both ways," she said softly, easing his worries as she reached out to pull his shirt off of him. "If I'm going to be naked and exposed in front of you, then you have to do the same." She stripped off his jeans and boxer briefs.

Distracting him with a little appreciative exploring, she managed to maneuver their positions so she was straddling his legs. "Because I don't want casual either, Brian. I want the raw, unboxable thing we have between us—emotional scars, stubborn-ass alpha tendencies and all."

And she meant it. She wanted him untamed, as untamed as he made her feel.

When she rocked her core against him and felt him pulse back—hot, hungry, and impatient—she *almost* gave in and abandoned her wicked plan altogether.

Almost.

Instead, she shifted forward, effectively taking a slick ride across his steel hard length just as, oops, her nipple slid past his lips...not exactly a difficult target considering he was gaping at her now in near desperate disbelief.

Fitted as tightly against him as she was, it took just one tiny little clenching of her inner muscles...

To find herself flipped onto her back.

"You evil little tease."

Her chuckle of laughter quickly turned into a demanding moan as she felt his teeth dole out his retaliation. A barely tamed nip that sensitized her nipple to near pain and—good lord—a tight, wet suction that had her legs clamping down around his waist.

"Oh no you don't," he grumbled roughly, gripping her ankles and pushing her knees back against the bedspread. Molten hot kisses rained down her torso as he hooked her legs hooked over his wide shoulders

A gliding lick and a rumbling groan were the next and last things she remembered before he stole her mind and hijacked her senses. Two thick unrelenting fingers—oh god, make that three—had her talking gibberish, mostly. Threats, definitely.

Clearly, the vindictive man was setting out to damn well *catapult* her over the edge.

...Or maybe not.

"*Brian!*" she cried out in a crazed frenzy.

Steel arms wrapped tight around her as his lips came down to claim hers. Then his rough, calloused hands were everywhere at once, memorizing every inch of her, branding her for him alone.

Yes. This was what she wanted. Brian unplugged.

Mindless with need, she shifted so he was nudging up against her now, just barely slipping in. Just a little deeper—

He tore his lips from hers. "Condom, Tessa. Now, dammit. I'm about two seconds from taking you without one."

"It feels better when you rub against me without one," she said without thinking.

"*Jesus Christ.*"

She angled her hips again, gliding against him until he

slid right over—

She gasped.

Once, she told herself, just once. She plunged down on him and reveled in how different it felt from the other night. Slicker, more sensitive. Hotter.

The slide back out was just as mind-erasing.

"That's it," he grated out before flipping her onto her stomach and sliding his hands under her with unerring aim. His teeth caught her earlobe just as his hands began issuing a no-holds-barred twin assault on her body.

Oh God.

She felt one of his hands abandon the mission a split second before his biceps flexed against her sides and a pillow was slid under her belly.

Then the hand was back.

But on its own mission.

The dual sensations were too much. She bucked against him when his lips laid scalding hot kisses across her back. Her hands nearly shredded the comforter when he grasped her hips and slid into her in one hard thrust.

All the way to the hilt.

And she exploded around him.

❦

HOLY HELL, the things he wanted to do to this woman. It'd never been like this for him. Wild and soul-deep, swimming in untamed emotions he couldn't name, didn't want to control. He relished every soft, needy sound he could drag out of her, imagined taking her against the wall, on her knees, in every way possible.

One more. Even though she was still pulsing all around him, riding out her last orgasm, he wanted her to lose control for him one more time.

Raking his teeth over her shoulder blade, he nipped at one creamy shoulder as he plunged into her again. Thrusting deep, he gripped her tighter, rode her harder until she began writing in his arms, needy, wrecked whimpers spilling from her lips.

She cried out his name as she shattered through her release, and a splintered bolt of lust shot through him, stole all semblance of restraint, of control. He surged inside her one last time, his orgasm twisting all through his body as wave after burning hot wave of intense pleasure crashed over him.

Decimated him.

Utterly ruined him for all other women.

CHAPTER THIRTEEN

TESSA BROUGHT OVER two plates of scrambled omelets and sat down across from him.

After nine days of spending every single night together, Brian was starting to come around to the breakfast food at dinner thing.

The gorgeous company, too.

Grinning as she clinked forks with him, he dug in, pausing only when he felt her eyes studying him. "Everything okay?"

"That's just what I was about to ask you. You look...I don't know...troubled."

So much for not worrying her.

He sighed. "It's Skylar. But don't freak out. She's fine."

Tessa put her fork down. "Then what's bothering you?" Concern darkened her eyes.

He loved how protective she was about her. "Nothing like the last time, I swear. She's just been a little down lately, and I think part of it is because Becky's decided she wants to try out for the volleyball team when they get to high school next year. It was bound to happen. They couldn't share every single extracurricular interest. Anyway, Becky's signed up for volleyball workshops every weekend afternoon for the next few weeks, so Skylar's a little bummed about that."

"Aw, poor girl."

"So, I've been trying to think of something special I can do. Nothing fancy, just maybe a father-daughter outing or something to cheer her up."

Suddenly, Tessa's eyes widened and a slow twinkle grew brighter and brighter in their depths.

Oh boy, this was going to be good. "Alright, tell me. What are you thinking?"

"It's a really good idea." She grabbed her laptop from the couch and brought it back to pull up some info. "Perfect for a father-daughter outing."

"Uh huh. I'll be the judge of that."

"You might hate it a little bit."

"I think we can safely change that 'might' to 'probably.'"

"*You* would've loved to do something like this at her age."

"*Aaand*, we can officially log this in the definitely hating it category."

"It involves a really pretty beach."

That brought his guard down a bit. "Skylar loves beaches."

"I know. She lights up whenever she talks about the beach. She even showed me her collection of sea glass once. I've never seen anything like 'em." Spinning her laptop around to face him, she could hardly contain her glee. "Okay, here it is. Check it out. Beautiful, right?"

He studied the pictures on the website and read the captions. "Pismo Beach? Yeah, it looks great. But it's like eight hours away. There are closer beaches."

Her shoulders were practically parked up next to her ears, her fingers flitter-clapping away before she went back to clacking away on the computer. "But *this* beach is special."

God, the woman had this uncanny ability to look hella sexy and crazy cute at the same time. He was all indulgent smiles for her when she spun the laptop back around to him again.

His grin faded. Okay, so right now, she was just plain crazy. "Are you out of your mind?"

"It's totally safe! Look, there's a kid doing it in that picture right there."

"Coastal dune ATV riding? You want Skylar to race up and down sand mountains in a quad?"

"Yesss. Oh, c'mon, look how fun it looks! And this is one of the few dunes that you can ride all the way down to the water."

It *did* look pretty cool.

She was practically buzzing out of her seat. "You know Skylar would love this."

No doubt.

"I don't know," he frowned. "Eight hours is still a long drive for a day trip."

Her face fell. "That's true."

"But I bet if you drove us, we'd get there in seven."

The look on her face was priceless. "What? No. I couldn't. This is your father-daughter outing."

"Which would be infinitely more special for Skylar if you came along." He scooted forward and popped a kiss on her lips. "For me, too."

Her smile went up to thousand-watt brilliance as she launched herself onto his lap and peppered his face with kisses. "I've always, always wanted to do this."

Laughing, he nuzzled the side of her neck, her bouncing hips in his lap sending his imagination heading in a completely new direction of one other thing he's always wanted to do. Settling her flush against him, he whispered against her lips. "You know what piece of furniture we haven't christened in this apartment yet?"

His imagination was having a field day already.

She hopped off his lap. "Rain check!" she called out as she ran off to her room. "There's so much to do before this trip." She practically cartwheeled all the way down the hall. "My first vacation."

With a sighing chuckle, he turned back around to finish eating his breakfast-dinner, smiling over the thought of taking her on her first non-work trip.

"Brian, I need your help for a second."

He went over to the bedroom. And got rock hard in an instant.

"It occurred to me," said Tessa as she draped two different bikinis on the desk chair that normally sat in the corner of her bedroom, "since I've never been swimming before, I've never actually worn a bathing suit. I bought these years ago, but never had a chance to wear them outside of the store."

For Brian, he had somehow gotten transported to a silent-movie place. With all the blood in his brain rushing past his ears and heading south, all he could do was watch, his eyes taking in every single detail before him.

The bikinis themselves were actually pretty tame. The naked woman standing there, holding them up against her body, however, was far less so.

She slowly rounded the chair and kept her back to him as she tied one of the bikini tops on.

Somehow, even though this was going terribly in reverse, it was sexy as hell.

Peeking over her shoulder at him, she reached for the matching bikini bottom and teased impishly with the worst—and still stunningly effective—pick-up line he'd ever heard, "If I dropped this rain check. Would you help me pick it up?"

Good lord, but he was falling head over heels in love with the woman.

∽∾

"THAT WAS THE BEST day *ever*!"

Brian chuckled, looking up at the rearview mirror and seeing Skylar nowhere near coming down from the excited high she'd been on since spending the day ATV riding at

Pismo Beach.

"And it was so gorgeous! I can't believe they let us drive all the way up to the shore. It was crazy! Can we come back again, dad? Pleeeease? Oh! And with an RV next time, so we can camp out on the sand dunes like all those other riders? I totally want to try one of the other quads too, like the ones the older kids were riding." She sighed happily. "I'm going to show Becky all the photos as soon as we get home. She's going to flip out. OMG, can we bring Becky next time, too?! That'll be *so* amazeballs!"

"Amazeballs?" mouthed Tessa, laughing silently.

Brian rolled his eyes. Yes, that seemed to be Skylar and Becky's current saying of choice. Personally, nothing he's done has warranted the prestigious honor until now. And now that it had, he was starting to come around on the word.

While Skylar continued to jabber and squeal in the back as she looked through the photos they'd taken throughout the day trip, Brian reached over and grabbed Tessa's hand, giving it a gentle squeeze. "Thank you," he said quietly, bringing her knuckles up to his lips.

They'd been driving for nearly three hours, and Skylar had been talking for about two and a half of it. It was really great to have his daughter back.

When finally nothing but deep breathing echoed out from the backseat, he looked and saw Skylar was fast asleep.

"This was all you, Tessa. I think I'm going to go in the dad hall of fame for this one."

"You're already in it," replied Tessa sleepily as she too

started to drift off to sleep. "In my book, and in Skylar's, you're definitely already in it."

She stifled a giant cat-yawn. "Maybe we should stop for coffee. I can't seem to keep my eyes open."

"Go on and sleep, babe."

"No," she protested weakly. "Then I'm going to be wired when we get home, and I'll be up all night listening to you snore in my ear."

His heart leapt up to his throat the moment he heard her say the word *home*. She'd never done that before, even by accident. The only home he'd ever heard her reference was her childhood home that she'd lost to foreclosure because she'd been unable to keep up the payments alone during her father's endstage. She'd only ever say 'my place' or 'my apartment' or 'your house.' But never, simply, 'home.'

With an intensity that truthfully stunned him a little, he wanted to hear her say it again, keep saying it.

Forever.

BRIAN WAS STILL closing the front door when Skylar dropped her backpack on the ground and bee-lined it straight for the cordless.

"Hold it!" he called out. "Laundry hamper and shower first, missy. You're getting sand everywhere and everything you're wearing is somehow still damp from the ocean." Could be because the girl had spent an hour driving the quad through the shore line like it was a jet ski on four wheels. "You can call Becky afterward."

With a mock salute, Skylar rushed down the hall and called out on her way to her room, "If Becky's not doing anything, can she come over later?"

"Did you finish all your homework?"

Silence.

Brian sighed and shook his head. "How about you tell Becky to bring her homework with her and then you two can pretend to study while you tell her about the trip. Then, afterward, you two can study for real with pizza as an incentive."

"Deal!"

Tessa wrapped her arms around his waist. "Nicely done. It's always impressive to see a hall-of-famer at work."

So she remembered that. He wondered if she remembered the rest of what she'd said in the car, too.

He brought her in for a kiss. "We should hurry and shower too. Do you want to save some electricity *and* water by—"

She clapped her hand over his mouth and gave him the cutest little scowl. Adorable rabbit. Even though Skylar was ecstatic that they were dating, Tessa was always extra mindful when Skylar was in the house. No showering together—especially not in the dark—no PDAs, and no sleepovers.

Though he was starting to wear her down on the latter two.

As Tessa ambled away to take a shower in his master

bath—alone—he noticed a cell phone on the ground near her bag, but not a smartphone. A flip phone that he didn't recognize. "Tessa? Do you have two cell phones?"

Tessa froze, patted her pockets quickly and spun around to check his hands. Eyes zooming in on the phone, she rushed over to swipe it from him.

"I found it on the ground; it must've fallen out of your pocket. Did you drop it while you were riding? It's got a big crack in it."

That seemed to alarm her even more. Frantic now, she flipped the phone open and began madly hitting the keys.

"Sweetheart, what's wrong?"

"I shouldn't have taken it with me," she cried out softly, sobbing as she fell to the floor. "But I wanted to take her with me."

That made absolutely no sense to him. But he didn't think this was one of her cute eccentricities. Seeing tears streaming down her face for the first time, true and real panic filled his veins, and he raced over to pull her into his arms.

"Tessa, honey, tell me what's going on, please. Let me help you. Is it your phone? Because if it's broken, we can fix it or replace it."

"I can't replace it. And it was already broken."

More incomprehensible answers.

"Talk to me, baby. Please."

"It was the last thing I had left."

Oh god.

Tessa was curled in a ball against his chest, clutching the

phone to her heart. "It's an old phone that doesn't work anymore, but it's the only thing I had left that still had Willow alive in it." Tessa opened it again and pressed at the buttons. Slowly, carefully this time, staring at the screen as if it would light up any second now.

It broke his heart when the phone didn't turn on.

"Now I've lost her forever." Hot tears slipped down her cheeks. "Willow was the *only one* who used to remember my birthday. Did I ever tell you that? The only one. Every year, my mom would forget…or rather, she just didn't remember because she never bothered to. My dad, on the other hand, would remember when he could, but he was usually bone tired from working all day in construction, and all night as a handyman that it'd usually just end up being an apologetic, belated wish, weeks later."

"But every single year, Willow remembered. Even with everything she was going through, even if she was in the ICU, she'd always, always remember and wish me a happy birthday." She cradled the phone in her hands and held it up to her chest. "The year Willow's memory started going, she'd taken my phone from my bag and told me to leave it with her for the day. I figured she was going to have the nurses help her bedazzle it or something so I didn't think anything of it. In fact, when I found it the next day on her nightstand looking exactly the same, I'd forgotten that she'd wanted it for some reason. I didn't remember until I got the ping on my calendar the next year. Willow's dementia had fully set in by then so she hadn't remembered it was my birthday, and I was prepared for that. But when I got that ping on my phone, I started bawling like a baby."

Tessa looked up at him, a trembling smile peeking through her tears. "Willow had left me a calendar entry to wish me a happy birthday for the following year, knowing her disease would make her forget. And not just that, but she'd included a little note as well on the calendar agenda. A note she knew I'd love."

"For years, Willow and I used to dream up these fantastic trips that we'd take together. We'd imagine that there was some miraculous cure for Huntington's and she'd be all better so we could travel the world. And as the years passed and our dreams got bigger, we started borrowing books from the library and checking out specials on TV and the internet—anything to learn about these far-off places."

Tessa shook her head, remembering something only she could see. "On that birthday calendar note, Willow had listed Greece as our dream destination of the day and eating our way through the country as the getaway goal we'd discussed." Eyes closed, she said softly, "And just like that, it was like she was right there with me again, dreaming with me."

She smiled in fierce, sisterly pride. "The truly amazing part was that by that year, Willow's hands were almost completely rigid, similar to Jilly's. So I can only imagine how long it took her to input all of those words." Tessa's fingers ran over the phone again. "It wasn't until the following year that I discovered it probably took her a whole lot longer than I'd imagined. There was another message that year. And then another the year following. Nine years now, and the calendar pings haven't stopped. I've gotten a birthday note from Willow every year since, and for that one day a year, we've traveled all over the globe together—boated around New Zealand, visited hot springs in Japan..."

Trailing off, she said softly, "I don't actually know how many she input. Never wanted to look and ruin the surprise. Instead, I just bought dozens of new batteries and made sure to keep the phone stored safe, even after a lot of the phone's other functions stopped working five years ago. I usually only taken it out of storage on my birthdays."

Her voice crumbled. "This Pismo Beach trip...it was the first vacation trip of my life and I wanted her to share it with me. So I brought the phone with me. To keep her close on our first real getaway adventure. I even thought about putting my own calendar note as a new memory. The first new memory we'd have together. ATV racing in Pismo beach." She buried her face against his chest and wept. "It was stupid."

Brian held her tight. "No, honey. It wasn't. It was beautiful. She would've loved it. For nine years, she's taken you around the world. And today, you got to take her."

"But now the phone is broken for good," she whispered in agony. "When those calendar pings would come each year, for that whole day, I'd be able to see her face crystal clear in my mind, and hear her voice as if she was sitting right next to me. It's like I had her back, like she was alive again for one day every year in this phone. And it was just for me. My one little birthday present. The only one I'd get, from the only person really who ever cared to remember and celebrate my being born."

Claws of pain and sympathy squeezed over his throat.

"Now she's finally gone. And even though I've had no family for nearly a decade, this is the first time I feel like I'm truly, completely alone in the world."

The last confession came out as a hoarse murmur and dissolved into broken tears.

He held her tight and just let her cry. Smoothing her hair back, he asked gently, "Tessa, what can I do?"

She answered quietly, almost numbly, "Can you take me back to my apartment please?"

Pain lanced at his heart. "Anything but that, honey. There's no way I'm leaving you alone by yourself."

"Please, Brian. I know you think I'm so strong but I'm not always. Not now. Not over this. I just want to go to bed. Escape for a while. Cry myself into tomorrow and hope it hurts just a little bit less come morning."

She looked like she was hanging on by the thinnest of threads. When another heartbreaking tear slid down her cheek, he finally relented, "Okay, sweetheart. Just let me make a quick call first."

A half hour later, he was in Tessa's bed, holding her under the covers and silently providing what little comfort he could until she eventually fell asleep.

He'd asked Abby to watch Skylar for the night so he could stay with Tessa. That was the only way he was going to let her stay here. But if it were up to him, they wouldn't be here at all. Her bedroom was worse than her living room. It wasn't a home. The room was perfectly functional, yes, but it lacked the warmth that a home should have, the warmth born and bred by family.

Thinking of Tessa's family brought him right back to the one person in her family that wasn't plagued with HD. Tessa's mother. God, his stomach felt like it was being sent through a meat grinder every time he thought about what her mother had forced upon her when she'd been even younger than Skylar was now, how she'd treated Tessa then and continued to treat her now.

The fact that Tessa had turned into the strong, amazing woman she was just made him all the more impressed with her, in awe of her.

That much more in love with her.

And that fact was what made bringing her back here so much tougher. She didn't belong here in this apartment. Not anymore. She deserved a *home*. She deserved a family so she didn't feel like she was alone in the world.

And more and more, he wanted that home and family to be one they shared together.

CHAPTER FOURTEEN

TESSA WAS BEAT.

It'd been a grueling week, one that she hadn't been ready to face after her meltdown last weekend. She'd had three grant proposals rejected on Monday, and discovered that one of her freelancers had submitted an 'accidentally' plagiarized piece on Tuesday. The clean-up for that had been hell. Then to add insult to injury, she'd caught a nasty bug midweek that had made the entire rest of the week move at a snail's pace. Now that it was finally the weekend, part of her just wanted to crawl into bed and sleep the day away, but thankfully, the rest of her was running on fumes and excitement as she finished up the dish she was taking over to Brian's house for the picnic Skylar had planned for today.

Never having been to a picnic before, the invitation had been the one bright point in Tessa's week. And spending the whole morning making one of the desserts that could always make her smile—even when she felt she couldn't—had actually left her feeling almost like her old self by the time afternoon rolled around.

After parking in the driveway behind Connor's Charger, Tessa went around to the side gate to head out into Brian's backyard. The sizzle of the grill and chorus of chatter greeted her like a warm summer wave.

"Ooh, ooh, she's here!" Skylar jumped up to give her a runaway train hug. "Okay, now we can officially start the picnic!"

Brian came over and slid his arm around. "Skylar apparently has an announcement she wants to make before we start eating. And she didn't want to start until you got here—she said she wanted her whole family to hear it."

Family. Tessa looked around at the sea of happy faces. Brian and Skylar, Skylar's grandparents, Connor and Abby, Becky and her parents and siblings.

Yes, this was definitely a family. One that Tessa would be honored to be a part of, in whatever capacity.

"Alright kiddo, you're up," called out Brian, giving the floor to Skylar.

"Hi everyone!" Skylar waved. "Okay, I know everyone's been really worried about me so I wanted to make a small announcement. Over the last couple of weeks, I got to talk with so many amazing, inspiring kids and adults who are living with HD." A small smile was directed Tessa's way. "All of them are out there living, dreaming, and fighting. Making the most of their lives...more than I've been making of mine lately." Her voice sobered a little. "Here I am, spending so much time thinking about what *might* happen *if* I have the HD gene when there are kids out there who've told me they only dream about having everything that I have. The 'normal' life I haven't really appreciated."

She took in a deep breath. "That's why I don't want to do it anymore. I want to focus on living, and being a kid. It doesn't make sense to waste a whole lifetime being afraid of my disease instead of being happy with my life. These kids I met can't have a 'normal' childhood but so far, I can. I've just been to stuck on the what-ifs to see that. And I don't think it's fair to all my new friends—or myself—if I didn't live my life to the fullest, without worrying about the HD gene until I absolutely have to. So..." a strong smile spread across her face, "*for now*, I've decided *not* to do the genetic testing."

Tessa's hand flew to her chest. For her, it had never been about whether Skylar took the test, not really, but rather, whether or not Skylar came to the decision on her own.

"To be honest, I of course still do really want to know," continued Skylar, "and I'll probably change my mind one day. But for right now, I want to live my life. I'm not going to waste my time worrying or being angry and sad as much anymore. I want to do the opposite—help more and get involved too like my Uncle Connor and Tessa do. As much as I can."

Her gaze spanned the yard, loving looking at all the people in her life. "Also, I really, really want to fall in love one day. And not just because driving my dad crazy when I start dating will be super funny."

Brian groaned, while everyone else laughed. But even so, there was a smile on his face. And profound pride in his eyes.

"So anyway, that's all. Just wanted to share my decision with all of you because you're all why my life is so happy to begin with. Okay, let's eat!"

A burst of applause sounded around the yard and Tessa just looked around at it all.

Brian wrapped his arms around her middle. "You did this. You helped her get her life back; you helped me get my daughter back."

"No. She did it all on her own. That is one special, amazing little girl you have there."

⚜

BRIAN LOOKED OVER at his animated daughter, watched as she walked around to greet everyone. This was the happiest he'd seen her in months.

And for the first time in a long while, *he* felt like he could breathe again.

Out of the corner of his eye, he finally noticed that Tessa had a big casserole skillet and a tiny little cooler on the ground beside her so he quickly moved to grab it. "I'll go put these on the table for you." He peeled back the foil and stared down at it. "What is it?" It looked like a cinnamon rolls, but he swore he smelled garlic.

Tessa smiled. "It's one of my specialties. Sweet garlic French toast roll with shiso ice cream."

A slow, cricket-friendly silence unrolled across the yard.

"Garlic *what* with *what* kind of ice cream?" asked Skylar, peering down at the dish in something akin to fear.

"I make a sweet dough similar to a cinnamon roll but instead of cinnamon, I use ground garlic with the sugar and butter. Then I roll it, bake it, and let it sit in a French toast batter," explained Tessa. "After that, I transfer the whole thing into a square skillet and bake it again—so it almost comes out like a bread pudding on the bottom half. Dust it with powdered sugar and a bit of garlic powder. Then I usually serve it with my shiso ice cream drizzled with honey and caramelized condensed milk." When everyone continued to stare at her, she chuckled and reassured them, "It's good, I promise."

"Okay, I have to try that," said Abby. "Bring it here."

The skillet was swooped out of Tessa's hands by Skylar, and the small cooler at Tessa's feet was liberated from her as well, this time by Becky.

"But...it's dessert," protested Tessa. She looked at Brian. "I swear, it's a sweet dish, not a savory one. It's not like garlic bread."

He chuckled. "Oh, don't worry, they get that. With Becky here, the sugar twins become three-prong-strong as the sugar triplets. They can eat dessert before, during, and after meals."

Everyone silently watched as Abby put a huge forkful of the roll, and the accompanying green ice cream, all covered with the gooey caramel and honey in her mouth. A few slow chews later and the groan of culinary bliss that split the air had them all rushing forward to grab bowls and heap on servings as well.

Tessa, meanwhile, just stood there staring at the crazy activity going on all around her, blinking in wonder.

"You okay, sweetheart?" he asked her, brushing a gentle kiss on her cheek to break her from her trance.

"I've never had this before," she murmured quietly.

Brian smiled. "What a rabid clan of folks fighting for the last piece of food?"

She laughed and shook her head. "A family." Gazing at Skylar, she added almost reverently, "Skylar is so lucky to have a family like this. HD gene or not, she's going to be just fine."

He wrapped his arms around her, wanting to ask her then and there if she wanted a lifetime membership to join their crazy family…when suddenly, they heard an ear-splitting scream from Skylar. They both spun around and saw Abby clap her hand over her mouth.

Tessa rushed forward. "Ohmigod, is something wrong with the dessert?" She was already grabbing the paper towel roll so Abby could spit it out.

"No, no," cried out Skylar, jumping up and down as she turned to Abby and nodded vigorously. "Tell them."

"Honey," said Abby quietly, "today was *your* big announcement day."

Skylar rolled her eyes. "OMG, if you won't tell them, I will!"

"Tell us what?" broke in Brian, his expression caught between concern and confusion.

Abby sighed, even though her eyes were dancing with excitement. "Skylar overheard me saying to Connor that I'm probably going to be asking him to haul Tessa over here to make this for me when I have my 3 a.m. pregnancy cravings."

Stunned, Brian's head whipped between Connor and Abby. "Pregnancy?"

Connor nodded, his expression that of pure proud-papa joy.

Brian rushed over to scoop Abby up in a huge python squeeze. "Holy shit! Congratulations you two!"

With a quick look of concern, Connor stepped forward. "Careful, man. Easy with the incredible hulk hugs."

Plopping a kiss on Abby's forehead before turning to his brother and yanking him up into a big bro-hug, Brian chortled, "Dude, it's not like I can shake the baby out of her."

"He's been like this for months," complained Abby, with an adoring head tilt in Connor's direction.

"*Months?*" bellowed Brian then. "How far along are you?"

"About four and a half months."

The timeline immediately made him think of Abby's first pregnancy. Looking over at his brother, Brian asked quietly, "Is everything…"

"Great so far," confirmed Connor. "The baby is growing like crazy. Abby's HCG levels and everything have been great so her doctor is optimistic so far about the viability. Plus, we have specialists who've talked us through the different ways we can help the pregnancy along. There's so much more technology now that wasn't available when Abby was a teen, so we're doing everything we can to monitor her and the baby."

"And Connor has, of course, been treating me like I'm made out of glass the entire time. I can't even lift a finger without him having a fit."

Relieved over the reassuring news, Brian eased back into his teasing and gave his brother a horrified expression. "Bad idea, man. Abby and pampering do not mix. I made that mistake once when she got the flu in college. It was diva city for the next month," he lied, chuckling at Abby's indignant scowl, which was no doubt because the exact opposite had been the case.

"Connor, honey. Can you come over and lift my middle finger for me please?" asked Abby prettily.

Brian burst out laughing and gave the happy parents-to-be another round of hugs before letting everyone else get in their hugs and congrats in as well.

It didn't register for Brian until a short while later that the *SilverHawks* theme song had been ringing in the air during the loud merriment that had followed Abby's announcement.

And that Tessa was no longer in the yard with them.

CHAPTER FIFTEEN

CONNOR WINCED as he looked out his office door and saw Brian storming down the hallway. He immediately hit his intercom button. "It's fine, Laura. You can let him in."

Brian barged into Connor's office and slammed his hands down on his desk. "Where the hell is she?"

"For the last time, I still don't know, man. Honest to God."

"Why aren't you worried? If it were Abby that was missing, you'd have had Jay and your firm's entire investigative team on it from the second you noticed her gone."

True.

"But Brian, Tessa isn't missing. She's been contacting you. Hell, she's been in contact with all of us."

"She hasn't been at her apartment in days!" Brian roared. "It makes no friggin' sense. She's getting all her work done online but no one knows where she's staying. And the only thing she keeps telling everyone, me included, is that she needs a little time to take care of a few *important* things. I swear to God, that woman is a walking flight risk. When I find her, I'm going to chain her to my damn bed for good."

Holy shit. This was *not* the calm, easygoing brother he'd known all his life. "What the hell has gotten into you?"

"She has! Not that I can say the reverse is true. The woman refuses to let me in, to let me help her."

"Brian, maybe she doesn't need your help."

Suddenly, the anger just fizzled right out of Brian like hot air out of a balloon. "Then what good am I to her?"

"*What?*"

"Beth and Abby, they had always needed me. Tessa just plain doesn't. She's proven it to me time and time again. She's been doing everything on her own for more years than I've even been responsible enough to take care of myself. She's survived more loss than I have, overcome more hardships, and achieved more feats—all without a family, without a home, without even friends, really. So what good am I to her? I may as well just be a casual fling for all the effect I have on her life."

Connor sighed. The nonsensical ramblings of a man blinded by a woman were always hard to listen to. "Do you love her?"

"I love her past sanity. It defies reason or caution. It trumps…everything. She thinks, and I know you do a little bit too, Connor, that she's everything I should avoid. Just because she has HD. Because of my past and her future. But what everyone fails to understand is that Tessa is everything I can't live without. Everything I *refuse* to live without."

Surprised—or stunned, more like—Connor sat there and studied his brother's turbulent expression. Brian looked positively savage, like a man willing to go into battle. Hell, he looked ready to wage a war if need be.

For Tessa.

"Well then...go get her, man."

⁓⁓

"I HAVE A SURPRISE for you!" cried Jilly, clapping excitedly.

Grinning, Tessa went over to sit next to Jilly's bed. Since her flight back had been delayed four hours, she'd only had a quick minute to shower off the travel grime before booking it over to make sure she could get over to see Jilly before dinnertime—she'd already missed her normal half-day visit earlier in the week.

Helping to sort through the pile of things on Jilly's activity tray, she ventured a guess, "Did you draw another picture of me in the circus? Because I don't know if you're going to be able to outdo the one of me as a lion tamer—"

"Nope!" Jilly interrupted excitedly. "It's this!" She used her thumb to slide open her nightstand drawer and did a flamboyant *ta-dah* motion.

Tessa peered inside and found what looked to be a little cosmetic compact, except instead of a translucent powder within the normal human skintone range, it was bright, neon green.

"There's a note, too! Openit, openit!" buzzed Jilly in one long excited breath.

Puzzled, Tessa flipped open the note taped to the back. The note was in Brian's handwriting—or at least it looked like his handwriting, but it was actually legible.

It's hair dye chalk. Skylar told me about it. I went searching for the safest one on the market and checked with the nurses. They said this one is perfectly safe for Jilly to use. This way, both of you can color your hair neon green for the day.

I also included a disposable camera. Just in case you want to start collecting memories again. Figured a photo of you and Jilly w/ your green hair might go great with the one of you and your sister w/ your pink hair.

I really hope you do want to start collecting memories again, sweetheart, because I want to start collecting a lifetime of them with you.

I miss you.

"Do you like the surprise?" asked Jilly.

Tessa wiped a wayward tear from her eye. "More than you can possibly imagine, Jilly."

"Yaay! Then you'll LOVE all the others!" she squealed, pointing over at the window seat behind the TV cabinet. Her voice dropped to a reverent whisper. "Can we play with them later?"

Tessa turned around and just stared in shock at the sight

before her. It looked like a convention of '80s cartoon characters. An *Inspector Gadget* lunchbox, a whole bunch of stuffed *Care Bears* and *Smurfs*, a *Jem and the Holograms* dvd set, a *Rainbow Bright* coloring book, and the complete *SilverHawks* and *ThunderCats* action figure sets.

Good lord, she was hopelessly in love with that man.

"Brian brought all that for me?"

Jilly nodded vigorously. "Uh-huh! He came every day this week with a present for you." Then a scolding look passed over her face. "He was *not* happy when you weren't here. I think you made him sad, Tessa."

Ouch. Leave it to a six-year-old to put her in her place. "Yes, I think I did, too. Do you think he'll forgive me?"

Jilly sat and thought about that seriously for a moment. "I think if you go over there and apologize nicely, and give him a big hug *maybe* he'll forgive you."

Sometimes the classics really were the best.

The 'maybe' did have her a little worried though.

She leaned over and gave Jilly a loving peck on the forehead. "You are a genius. We'll color our hair green this weekend, okay? And take some pictures?"

"Okay," agreed Jilly cheerfully. "Remember now," she reemphasized as Tessa was leaving, "a BIG hug."

As she rushed out of the care home, Tessa pulled out her phone and dialed Brian's house number.

Answering machine.

Damn it.

His cell phone seemed to be ringing through though.

"Where the hell have you been, woman?"

Tears sprang into her eyes. Happy tears. For all of it—the protective alpha growl, the way he never said her name with a question mark when she called, and the love in his voice that had only grown since they'd last talked. Definitely happy tears.

"Hello to you, too."

"So does this phone call mean you're done running?" he asked gruffly.

"I didn't run!" she argued back hotly.

Really, she didn't.

"Where are you now?"

"I was headed over to see you, actually."

"Good," came the rough reply. "Then I won't have to let the air out of your tires."

Doing a double take, Tessa looked up and saw Brian leaning against her car, staring at her like a man possessed. Or at least a man in love with a woman who made him feel possessed.

She shoved her phone in her bag and launched herself into his arms. "I've missed you."

His arms snapped shut around her like steel bands. "Then you shouldn't have run," he grumbled against her hair, a low ragged exhale of relief following soon after.

"I didn't run!" she maintained pushing back to stand her ground. "I...hid."

A world of difference.

"You shouldn't have been hiding from me either, Tessa.

When are you going to get it into your stubborn little head that I want you? All of you—quirky habits, too-independent-for-your-own-good tendencies, HD gene and all. I've been giving you time, waiting for you to come to me. But you know what? Screw that. You're coming home with me. Home. With me. That's where your home is. Not that apartment. Not whereever the hell you've been for the last few days."

He took in a deep, jagged breath and cupped her cheek. "I know you're scared and I am too, sweetheart. But if Huntington's is going to steal your memories one day years and years from now, well then we'll just make its job that much harder and longer by filling our lives with more memories than it can take, fill that busy little head of yours so it takes years, decades to wipe out. Green hair, ATV trips, you name it, we'll collect an endless string of memories. Together."

She stared at him, her heart hammering, legs barely holding her up. "That could be the most romantic thing you've ever said to me."

"Really?" His voice graveled even more. "How about I do one better..." Dragging her back into his arms, he said gruffly, "Marry me. Be by my side to watch Skylar graduate from high school, and college, and whatever else she decides to do. Be by my side so she'll be inspired to go out and fall in love. But mostly, be by my side so I can be by yours too. Marry me, Tessa Daniels."

Heart swelling to double capacity, words were failing her

completely, oxygen too, for that matter.

"You don't have to rush on answering, sweetheart," he continued gently, "I'm not going anywhere. But one thing I do want to give you a heads-up on is that your mother knows already because I called her this week—not to *ask* for your hand, but to tell her I was damn well *taking* your hand in marriage."

Later, she'd process this all much more carefully but for now, all she could do was parrot back the most shocking of all the verbal grenades he'd just launched her way, "You called my mother?"

Funny, in her head, she was sure her mouth was going to ask the much more burning question: *You really want to marry me?*

"Yes. I had Jay find her phone number for me soon after you left. I was worried out of my mind and I decided to tell her off, basically. To tell her exactly what I thought about her. About how horrible she'd been to you. But instead, I ended up telling her exactly what I thought about *you* instead. How much I love you. How incredible you are, and how happy you've make me. How happy I want to make you in return for the rest of our lives."

Every ounce of love she had for the man lodged in her throat. "H-how did it go?" she finally managed.

"I think her voicemail was very moved," he replied roughly, looking thoroughly disgruntled. "I must have called her a hundred times and she never once answered her phone."

A soft laugh somehow found its way out of her. "My

mom screens all her calls on her cell phone. That's why I usually call her on her landline."

"I tried that, but her landline was disconnected."

"Right. That's because she moved. Or so I discovered when I flew out there this past week."

This time it was Brian's turn to be stunned. "You went to go see your mother?"

"Yes. That's the other thing I've been doing—and also why I was gone for those extra few days. I just...needed to. She wasn't at the address I had. Surprise, surprise, she sort of forgot to tell me she'd moved again. So I had to stay an extra few days to find her. I had no intention of leaving without seeing her." She shrugged. "And of course when I did manage to find her, it wasn't one of those movie endings. She was on her way to work and literally had only five minutes for me."

She felt her heart do a double-thump when Brian bristled and growled over that.

"It was okay though because five minutes was all I needed. I told her that I wanted her to see me in person. See that the daughter who'd begun dying in her mind the day the gene tests came back grew up to be a strong, happy woman. A woman who is living with HD and helping others with it. A woman not afraid to love and be loved. A woman who deserves to have a happily ever after with the man of her dreams, and look forward to the future instead of spending her life dreading it."

Blinding pride took over Brian's expression.

"I gave her two photos—the one of me with my dad and

Willow, along with the photo of you, me, and Skylar from our ATV trip. And I also gave her my phone number, laminated, and on a magnet...which I stuck on her fridge. So if she doesn't call, it's not because she doesn't have my number anymore."

Despite his obvious disgust with the woman, his expression held hope...for her.

Tessa shook her head. "She ushered me out of her apartment a minute later saying she'd be late for work. And that was the end of that reunion."

"Honey, I'm so sorry."

"I'm not. She is who she is, and I became who I am despite that."

He nodded and pulled her into his arms. "And despite her, you're going to become something she *never* was."

She tilted her face up to his. "What's that?"

He untucked a small gift bag from the cargo pocket of his jeans. "I've had this as your homecoming gift from the day I figured it all out." With a soft smile, he whispered, "Open it."

Something about the way he was looking at her... She looked in the bag and gasped when she saw the baby onesies in it. "*How?*"

"I guessed. I thought of the one thing that would make you run—"

"*I didn't run!*" she growled. "The day of the picnic, I'd stopped at the doctor's to make sure I didn't have a contagious bug. With Jilly and everyone else in the care home, we always need to be careful of that. He called me during the picnic to tell me the results of my blood test."

"And then you—"

She poked him viciously in the stomach. "I didn't *run*! I told you, I was hiding!"

"Meaning you were trying to hide the pregnancy from me?"

"*What?!* No! I spent the time setting up a trust with my father's life insurance money and then seeing prenatal genetic specialists to find out about the prenatal HD gene test. This way, when I told you, there wouldn't be any financial obligations for you to worry about, and I'd have all the info on the HD gene testing for you as well. That way, if you didn't..."

She couldn't finish the sentence.

And it was probably a good thing because something akin to shocked, violent outrage crossed his face.

"You thought I wouldn't want our child?!" he roared.

"No! I just... I have the HD gene—that means our child will have the same fifty-fifty chance too. I just wanted to do everything I could so you *could* walk away if you wanted to, and have all the gene info ready for you if you only wanted to walk away...in certain conditions," she finished lamely.

With him just glaring at her, likely counting to ten silently, she rambled on, "You can find out for sure before agreeing to be a part of the pregnancy. There are two prenatal genetic tests; the one that's later in the pregnancy is a little safer but—"

"Don't do the testing." His voice had finally calmed and his eyes had warmed first with quiet, uncontainable excitement, and then with affectionate empathy.

The combination, along with his quiet statement had her shaking like crazy—sheer and naked hope being as potent as adrenaline when it was rushing through your veins.

"Are you sure, you don't want to—"

"Sweetheart, really. Don't do it. We don't need the added danger to you or the baby."

"But don't you want to know? I mean with me, and Skylar…"

"Tessa, it wouldn't matter what the prenatal gene test said. At least not to me." His frame stiffened. "Are you thinking of terminating the pregnancy based on the results?"

Horrified, she gasped in outrage. "Of course not!" She glared at him. "Would you still want to marry me if it were positive?"

He tugged her in close and rumbled against her lips. "Of course I would."

She smiled and relaxed. "So we're really doing this?"

"Yes. Now take a better look at your present. I think they're friggin' cute as hell and I've been holding on to them for days, dying to see your face when you saw them."

Her heart melted into a puddle of goo.

She opened the bag and broke out into a huge grin as she pulled out the little novelty onesies he'd bought. "He-Man and She-Ra?" she chuckled.

"Yep. I know we won't know what the gender of the

baby is for months but I wanted to get both just in case. We can return the other or give it to Abby and Connor for their kid if the gender is right."

She bit her lip to hide the gigantic smile that was trying to break free. "Actually, it might be a good idea to keep both. Just in case we're having a boy *and* a girl."

At the slow shock blooming across his grin, she confirmed, "Because we're having twins."

EPILOGUE

"YOU READY TO GO on our honeymoon, sweetheart?"

Tessa giggled. "Did you see the look on everyone's faces when we told them what we were doing for our honeymoon?"

"Yes," Brian chuckled. "And I'd pay good money to see it again."

He helped his gorgeous wife with her barely showing baby bump into the SUV. Meanwhile, the small group of their closest friends and family were waving and blowing bubbles.

"Oh! Did you remember to get the CD back?"

Precious thing. "Honey, I keep telling you, I've made over dozens of copies." And backed up the file in over ten places.

When she just kept right on staring at him, waiting for an answer, he replied lovingly, "Yes, I remembered to get the CD back."

She beamed.

It thrilled him to no end that she'd loved his little musical surprise for her today.

Since he'd wanted Tessa to have something truly special for their wedding day, he'd taken all of Willow's compositions and tracked down her old piano teacher, who'd been happy to play and record every single one.

And though Tessa hadn't heard the music in decades, she'd recognized it almost immediately when it came through on the speakers as the processional music for her walk down the aisle.

She'd burst into tears.

Happy tears, she later reassured him after he nearly had a heart attack and went racing up the aisle to get to her.

"I know you made copies of the CD. And I'm not being weird. *This* copy is from our wedding day. So I want to keep it as one of our keepsake memories from the ceremony. Of something my amazing husband did for me—and my sister."

He stilled for a surprised moment and then broke out into a grin. Per usual, Tessa was always surprising him. Not wanting to spend another second delaying their honeymoon, he quickly slid a kiss over her smiling lips and then ran around to the driver's seat.

And waited.

"What's wrong?" asked Tessa.

He checked his watch and opened the glove compartment, counting down.

3..2..1.

Her phone chirped.

Eyes dancing, she grabbed for the phone and went straight to her calendar.

He knew exactly what she'd find:

Happy Wedding Day
Where we'll go: Our Honeymoon
What we'll do: Go home and pitch your first tent in our backyard…clothing optional.

She burst out laughing, and the sound hit him square in the heart like it always did.

"Exactly how many of these calendar entries have you put in my phone?"

"Just the one," he said as he finally started up the car. "Because I intend to give you the rest of the reminders of how much I love you in person every day for the rest of our lives."

The End

Note From the Author

Fear not dear readers, you haven't seen the last of the Sullivans! My next series—three standalone novels and two novellas—takes place in that quirky little town of Cactus Creek I've been referencing throughout all the Nice Girl/Nice Guy books. Gosh, I love this place. I first 'created' this special, ruggedly beautiful town years ago; and since then, all my characters from the two series just up and decided it was the place to be. Though my muse and I tried to keep them from crashing each other's series, these defiant characters were not having it! Before I knew it, they were all becoming friends, hanging out together, and eventually butting into each other's lives with no regard for this author's sanity. *grin* Thus, it's safe to say that you can count on little cameos from the entire Nice Girl/Nice Guy gang throughout all the upcoming Cactus Creek series books.

The first Cactus Creek novel is:

Love, Chocolate, and Beer

Coming January 2014

Sneak Peek of *Rebel*
by
New York Times & *USA Today* Bestselling Author
Skye Jordan

-- Coming Summer 2014 --

All the Renegades were back, shrinking the trailer to the size of a thimble. Rubi could have choked on the testosterone thickening the air. But she was distracted.

Wes stood at the center of the room, the neoprene suit pulled off his shoulders, hanging low on his hips. She stopped short and slapped an open hand over her heart for the second time in fifteen minutes.

Her fantasies hadn't come close to the real deal, standing only six feet away. His denim blue eyes shone with residual excitement from that crazy-ass stunt. With his hands planted at his hips, his muscled pecs and biceps glistened with sweat. The fine line of golden hair low on his abdomen disappeared between his belly button and the waistband of whatever he wore beneath the neoprene. And every sexy muscle stood out in a relief of hills, planes and valleys.

He was freaking *carved*.

"Praise the gods of Olympus," she murmured, an ache developing deep at the center of her body.

He grinned, and his eyes twinkled with flirtation and heat.

He also had more ink than the simple tire treads circling

his left bicep and the stylized checkered flag flowing down his right calf. He had something covering his right shoulder, too.

"Is that..." she started, narrowing her eyes at the image, taking in the detail, the definition of shadow, the sheer artistic beauty of it, "a Terminator tatt?"

"Not exactly, but the same principle." Wes's gaze darted to his shoulder. "You like it?"

"What's a Terminator tatt?" Lexi asked.

Her friend's voice pulled Rubi's gaze from Wes. She frowned at Lexi, crouched on the floor behind him.

"What are you doing?"

"Fitting this..." --she huffed a breath as she struggled with something behind his back-- "to Wes."

Lexi stepped out from behind him, her hand running along a strip of metal against his thigh Rubi hadn't noticed, then lowered to her knees in front of Wes and repeated the move with deep concentration.

Rubi had seen her friend do this hundreds of times over the years while fitting wedding gowns or measuring for alterations. But today, something about witnessing it, while imagining herself in Lexi's place for a totally different reason, made the ache in Rubi's body spread lower.

She lifted her brows, grinning. "Might want to get off your knees before Jax comes in, Lex."

Wes's smile grew lopsided. "I'm totally down with you taking her place, Russo."

"Great idea," Lexi said glancing over her shoulder at Rubi. "Can you hold this so I can get a better look at the back?"

An absurd chuckle floated from her throat. "You've *got* to be kidding."

"What's the problem?" Wes challenged with that cocky grin. "Afraid you might like it?"

Irritation burned the back of her neck. The man knew she had a competitive streak. "I know what you're doing, Lawson."

One golden brow rose.

"Rubi," Lexi said, "we're not getting out of here until this is done."

"Fine." When she sauntered forward holding Wes's taunting gaze, Lexi stepped behind him. Rubi let the heat she used at the club slide into her grin. Maybe showing him a little more of her dark side would give him second thoughts about that earlier request for a date. "I guess it will be my undiluted pleasure…whether I want it or not."

Rubi pressed both hands flat against his bare chest. His skin was damp and warm and soft, the muscle beneath hard and radiating heat. A stream of liquid fire rolled through her body. His nipples tightened with her touch, stirring the craving she'd been restraining for weeks. She ran her tongue over her bottom lip, wishing she could stroke it across the deep brown nub.

As if Wes had the magical power of focus, everything outside her field of vision dimmed. Lexi's self-directed mutters melted into nothing. The other guys' chatter dissipated. The noise outside faded.

Even at five-nine, wearing three-inch heels, she had to tilt her head to look into his eyes. His gaze was heavy-lidded, but sharp, serious and scorching. Those full lips had lost their grin and his jaw ticked with pent up energy. There was definitely a more intense side to this easy-going country-boy—one that coaxed her interest and ramped her desire.

She balanced herself with pressure against his chest and slowly lowered. Keeping her gaze pinned to his, her hands slid down the hard wet muscle. God, he was utterly delicious.

Curling her fingers into the waistband of what she could see now were shorts beneath—*too bad*—she used his body to steady her as she rocked to her knees.

His gaze had transitioned into something primal. Something hungry. Predatory. Rubi let herself imagine what he'd do to her now if they were alone. How he'd slide his big hands into her hair, guide her mouth to his cock and draw her forward until he was buried to her throat. A telltale tickle signaled growing moisture between her thighs.

Speaking to Lexi while holding Wes's smoldering gaze, Rubi added heavy suggestion into her voice. "What do you need?"

A touch of satisfaction, of power, flicked one corner of his mouth.

Lexi grabbed Rubi's hands, moving them to a pair of round contraptions on either side of Wes's hips. "Hold these right there."

"Will do."

Wes let a hand fall toward her face. He traced the tip of one finger across her forehead and lifted a strand of hair, setting it aside. The move was so sweet, so intimate, a fist balled in her stomach.

"You look good right there, Russo," he said, his voice low, the thick heat wafting over Rubi's skin like warm air. "Really good."

His finger traced a tingling path down her cheek and across her jaw. Then his hand opened and his thumb swept the angle of her cheekbone. The sensation created such a decadent sensation inside her, Rubi had to fight to keep her eyes open.

"And you look good right there, Lawson." She forced her voice light to hold the teasing edge. Letting him know he unnerved her was not an option. "Really good."

Lexi pulled at something near the base of Wes's spine and his hips swayed closer to Rubi's face. His grin grew, and Rubi bit her lip against a laugh.

Footsteps sounded on the trailer's stairs. "Are we ready for lunch?"

Jax's question, clearly asked before he took in the scene, gave her laughter an escape route.

Wes pressed his thumb against the center of her lower lip, dragging her mouth open a little more, then murmured, "Just say the word…"

And I'll be your lunch.

He didn't need to say the words for her to know what he was thinking. What they were both thinking.

[*END OF EXCERPT*]

Sneak Peek of A Maine Christmas...Or Two
by
New York Times & USA Today Bestselling Author
J.S. Scott

and

Cali MacKay

-- Available Now --

This book contains two brand new, steamy, contemporary romance Christmas stories from NY Times and USA Today Bestselling author J.S. Scott and Cali MacKay. Although these stories are connected to both authors' current series, they are easily stand-alone reads with no cliff hangers.

The Billionaire's Angel
by J.S. Scott
(The Billionaire's Obsession Christmas Story)

Considered an eccentric beast by most of the residents in Amesport, Maine, Billionaire Grady Sinclair stays isolated on his private peninsula in a grand mansion most people are afraid to approach. The arrangement suits Grady just fine, until a fearless angel lands on his doorstep, making him painfully aware of how lonely he really is, and how much he wants to keep the fiery blonde cherub for his very own. But will he have to become the monster the townspeople believe him to be in order to get his Christmas wish?

Emily Ashworth needs money, and plenty of it. As director of the Youth Center of Amesport, she either finds the funds she needs to supply Christmas presents and other items she needs to purchase to give the kids of Amesport a Christmas, or they won't have one at all. Desperate, she ventures to the Amesport Peninsula to ask the wealthiest person in the area to provide a Christmas for her misplaced, abused, or troubled kids, and to help keep the doors of the much-needed refuge open. Emily is shocked when she meets Grady, and surprisingly more attracted to him than she has ever been to any man. He might have seemed like a barbarian in the beginning, but Emily quickly learns that Grady is nothing like she'd imagined. Was the monster of Amesport truly the very devil, or just a lonely man who needs the gift of love for Christmas?

A Mermaid Isle Christmas
by Cali MacKay

Once Aidan Nordson made his fortune, he was finally able to leave behind the world that left him broken and scarred. Escaping to Mermaid Isle, all he wants is to be left alone to live his life and deal with his demons, but when a blizzard hits and strands Chloe Madison at his door, the gorgeous and feisty brunette stirs feelings in him he'd rather push away. Forced together by fate and circumstance, can Aidan let go of the past that haunts him so he can learn to love again or will the storm in his heart swallow him in its darkness?

The Billionaire's Angel
(c) J. S. Scott

Emily couldn't see well, but she squinted into the swirling snow and pushed her glasses back up onto the bridge of her nose. Passing several private driveways, she kept on going, knowing Grady's home was the very last one.

The road ended at his house, and Emily forged ahead, parking her truck in the circular driveway and turning off the engine.

I must be insane!

Before she had time to think about what she was doing and leave, Emily grabbed her purse and slammed the door of the truck closed. Glad she was dressed in a sweater and jeans for the weather, she just wished she was also wearing a pair of boots, her sneakers slipping and sliding in the fresh, wet snow.

The house was massive, and she gaped at the heavy oak doors in front of her, wanting to run away as fast as her slippery shoes would take her.

"What kind of single guy owns a house this humungous?" she whispered in awe.

Answering herself, she said, "A man who has enough money to donate for the Youth Center."

With that thought in mind, she strode determinedly forward and pressed the doorbell harder than she needed to, causing her feet to slide out from under her and land ungracefully in a heap on Grady Sinclair's doorstep.

That was a fabulous and graceful entrance, Emily. Impress him with your professionalism.

Disgusted with herself, she scrambled for purchase on the icy stone porch, trying to hastily get to her feet before he answered the door, but she slid again and landed flat on her rear end, flinching as her tailbone hit the unyielding surface. "Damn!"

Abruptly, the door swung open, and Emily Sinclair got her first look at the beast from an undignified position on her frozen ass.

Her glasses were wet and foggy, but he looked like no beast she had ever seen. He did, however, look pretty fierce, dark, and dangerous. Without saying a word, Grady Sinclair stuck his hand out as though he completely expected her to take it. She did, grasping his hand as he pulled her to her feet like she was as light as a feather. Trying to straighten up quickly to regain some modicum of dignity, she gawked up at him. She was tall for a woman, but he dwarfed her, towering over her menacingly. He was dressed informally in a tan thermal shirt that stretched across rippling muscles and a massive chest. He was sporting a pair of jeans that looked worn, and he filled them out in a way she'd never seen a man wear a pair of jeans before.

Holy crap! Grady Sinclair was hot. Scorching hot. His dark hair was mussed, and he had a just-rolled-out-of-bed look that made her want to drag him back to a bedroom. Any bedroom. He looked like he hadn't shaved today, and the dark, masculine stubble on his jaw just added to the testosterone waves she swore she could almost feel pulsating from his magnificent body and entering hers, making her squirm just a little at her body's reaction to him.

She drew in a deep breath as his gray-eyed stare seemed to assess her, and finally came to rest on her face. "Hi," she said weakly, unable to form any intelligent words right at the moment. Her brain was mush and her cheeks flushed pink with mortification. This just wasn't the businesslike, graceful entrance she had hoped for, and her lustful reaction to Grady

Sinclair had her uncharacteristically flustered.

I need to get it together. I'm acting like an idiot. I need this donation.

He grabbed a fistful of her jacket and tugged her inside, closing the door behind her. Plucking the glasses from her face, he used his shirt to clean them before he handed them back to her. "You don't look like one of Evan's usual women," he said gruffly. "Bedroom is upstairs." He pointed his thumb toward the spiral staircase on the far side of the enormous front room.

Emily stared at him blankly for a moment, and then slanted her gaze toward the living room to try to clear her head. She certainly couldn't seem to think straight when she was looking directly at *him*.

Bedroom? What the hell is he talking about? Evan's women?

"I think you have me mistaken for someone else. I don't know you, and I'm not acquainted with Evan. I came to ask a favor." *Who does he think I am?*

"And you're offering *your* favors for a favor, right?" he asked grimly, his graveled baritone almost disapproving.

Her head jerked back to his face. "What? No. What kind of favor?" she replied suspiciously.

"My brother Evan told me I needed to get laid, which generally is followed by a woman arriving here at my house. I usually just send the women away with a check. But I've decided I'll take you," he said huskily.

Emily gulped. "Someone sends you women...as in prostitutes?" Good God, the last thing Grady Sinclair needed was a hooker. She couldn't think of one single woman who would actually turn him down. "Do I look like a whore?" she asked irritably, suddenly offended by the fact that he'd thought she was for sale. But she felt a shiver of need slide down her spine and land right between her thighs at the thought that he actually wanted her, and what he might do to her if she *was* actually a woman for hire. She wasn't beautiful and she was curvy, her ample figure a little more than most men found attractive.

He reached out and unzipped her jacket, divesting her of the garment and hanging it on a hook by the door. Turning back to her, he said slowly, "Nope. You don't. That's why I want to fuck you."

Emily gasped, his blatant words and heated appraisal making her flush. "Well, I don't know Evan and I don't want to do *that*." *Liar. Liar.* She so *did* want to do *that*, but she wasn't about to admit it when he'd just insulted her. Besides, she didn't do casual sex. "I'm Emily Ashworth and I'm the director of the Youth Center of Amesport. I wanted to talk to you about a possible donation."

She shuddered as his intense, molten gaze swept over her body and back to her face, staring at her with a look so smoldering and hungry that her core clenched in response.

"You're cold," he said abruptly, taking her frozen hand in his and leading her through the living room, down the hallway and into a cheery kitchen. "Sit," he demanded huskily as he dropped her hand, halting at the kitchen table.

Emily sat, so confused that she was unable to make herself do anything else. She watched silently as Grady Sinclair moved around the kitchen, his large body maneuvering with a fluidity of motion that shouldn't be possible for a man as large and muscular as he was. Watching him from behind was almost mesmerizing. She was jealous of the denim that was cupping an ass so tight that she could see the flex of muscle beneath the seat of his jeans as he moved, and it was a view she couldn't bring herself to look away from for some time.

Finally, ripping her gaze from him, she let her eyes wander around the kitchen—a bright, airy room with beautiful granite countertops and polished wood floors. Beyond, there was a dining room with a formal, polished wood table, but the room was dim, sparsely furnished, and looked seldom used.

He sauntered to the kitchen table moments later and pushed a mug in front of her, sitting down next to her with his own cup in hand. Emily placed her cold fingers around the mug, sighing as she inhaled the hot, fragrant brew. It was a hot apple cider, and she took a long sip, the warm liquid instantly starting to warm her. "Thank you," she told him quietly as she set her mug back on the table. "So will you consider it?"

"Why?" he questioned darkly, his heated gaze spearing her as she squirmed uncomfortably in her chair.

"The Center needs money."

"Why?" he asked again, lifting a brow as he sipped his drink, his eyes never leaving her.

He knows I'm desperate, that there's a reason I'm here so late asking for money.

"A man I was dating stole the operating money from the Center and we can't keep running without a significant donation," she admitted, wondering why she was feeling the need to be completely honest with him.

Starting hesitantly, she spilled the entire story about the money being stolen as Grady watched her, his expression unreadable as he listened. "So would you be willing to help?" she asked nervously as she finished her story.

He was silent, his expression contemplative as he continued to look at her. Intense minutes passed before he finally answered, "I might be willing to consider it. But I'd want something in return."

She picked up her mug and took another sip of cider, swallowing awkwardly before she spoke again. "What? I'll do whatever I can to get you what you want." The whole future of Amesport depended on his answer. Emily knew she had nowhere else to go and no other solution.

"That's good, because you're the only one who can get it for me," he agreed casually. "Because what I really want is *you.*"

Emily nearly choked, sputtering as she swallowed. Dear God, maybe Grady Sinclair *was* the Amesport Beast after all. "I need to give the town of Amesport a Christmas, they need the Center to stay open, and I'll do anything to keep from disappointing the kids there, but I'm not sleeping with you to do it," she told him indignantly.

"We don't need to sleep," Grady replied gruffly. "And I hate Christmas."

[*END OF EXCERPT*]

ABOUT THE AUTHOR

Violet Duke is the pen name of Nina Nakayama, lovingly chosen in honor of her two wacky children. Once a professor of English Education at the University of Hawai'i, Nina is ecstatic to now be on the other side of the page, writing wickedly fun contemporary romance novels while her muse alternates between perching on her left and right shoulder (usually left). When she's not catering to the whims of her story characters or feeding her book-a-day reading addiction, she enjoys tackling random reno projects with her power tools while trying pretty much anything without reading the directions first, and cooking 'special edition' dishes that laugh in the face of recipes. Nina lives in Hawai'i with her two cute kids and similarly adorable husband.

Visit her at:
http://www.violetduke.com

For up-to-date info and giveaways, become a fan at:
http://www.facebook.com/VioletDukeBooks
http://www.goodreads.com/VioletDukeBooks
http://www.twitter.com/VioletDukeBooks

Or send her an email (she loves hearing from fans!):
authorvioletduke@gmail.com

Other Titles By the Author

NICE GIRL TO LOVE (Serial Romance) Series

RESISTING THE BAD BOY, Book #1
Available Now

FALLING FOR THE GOOD GUY, Book #2
Available Now

CHOOSING THE RIGHT MAN, Book #3
Available Now

NICE GIRL TO LOVE: The Complete Collection
Available Now

FINDING THE RIGHT GIRL: A Nice *GUY* Spin-Off
Available Now

CACTUS CREEK Series

LOVE, CHOCOLATE, AND BEER
Coming January 2014

LOVE, WEAPONS, AND COMBAT
Coming May 2014

LOVE, SIDELINES, AND ENDZONES
Coming September 2014

Printed in Great Britain
by Amazon.co.uk, Ltd.,
Marston Gate.